T4-AJT-974

"DON'T YOU THINK YOU OWE ME AN EXPLANATION, CINDY?" NICK DEMANDED.

"Yes, of course I do. You see, I sometimes dress up like this, as Madame Destiny, to go to charity functions and—"

"Butt into people's lives," he said, interrupting her.

"No, I just read their palms and tell them—"

"Whatever strikes your fancy, regardless of the consequences."

"Nick, I didn't plan to deceive you. It just sort of happened. I meant to tell you the truth."

"Sure, you did," he replied with a dry, humorless laugh. "That's why you danced with me at the charity ball as Madame Destiny and fed me lines about how *perfect* 'Cindy' was for me." He glared at her and strode across the room to the door. "Well, read your own palm and see if it says that I'm fixing to walk out of your life forever. For once you'll be right."

CANDLELIGHT ECSTASY CLASSIC ROMANCES

WEB OF DESIRE,
Jean Hager

DOUBLE OCCUPANCY,
Elaine Raco Chase

LOVE BEYOND REASON,
Rachel Ryan

MASQUERADE OF LOVE,
Alice Morgan

CANDLELIGHT ECSTASY ROMANCES®

486 THE DRIFTER'S
REVENGE, *Kathy Orr*
487 BITTERSWEET
TORMENT,
Vanessa Richards
488 NEVER GIVE IN,
JoAnna Brandon

489 STOLEN MOMENTS,
Terri Herrington
490 RESTLESS YEARNING,
Alison Tyler
491 FUN AND GAMES,
Anna Hudson

QUANTITY SALES

Most Dell Books are available at special quantity discounts when pur-
chased in bulk by corporations, organizations, and special-interest
groups. Custom imprinting or excerpting can also be done to fit special
needs. For details write: Dell Publishing Co., Inc., 1 Dag Hammarskjold
Plaza, New York, NY 10017, Attn.: Special Sales Dept., or phone: (212)
605-3319.

INDIVIDUAL SALES

Are there any Dell Books you want but cannot find in your local stores? If
so, you can order them directly from us. You can get any Dell book in
print. Simply include the book's title, author, and ISBN number, if you
have it, along with a check or money order (no cash can be accepted) for
the full retail price plus 75¢ per copy to cover shipping and handling.
Mail to: Dell Readers Service, Dept. FM, P.O. Box 1000, Pine Brook,
NJ 07058.

DESTINY'S LADY

Kathy Clark

A CANDLELIGHT ECSTASY ROMANCE®

Published by
Dell Publishing Co., Inc.
1 Dag Hammarskjold Plaza
New York, New York 10017

Copyright © 1987 by Kathy Clark

All rights reserved. No part of this book may be reproduced or transmitted in any form or by any means, electronic or mechanical, including photocopying, recording or by any information storage and retrieval system, without the written permission of the Publisher, except where permitted by law.

Dell ® TM 681510, Dell Publishing Co., Inc.

Candlelight Ecstasy Romance®, 1,203,540, is a registered trademark of Dell Publishing Co., Inc., New York, New York.

ISBN: 0-440-11810-7

Printed in the United States of America

March 1987

10 9 8 7 6 5 4 3 2 1

WFH

This book is dedicated to the most wonderful in-laws a woman could have, A. C. and Bertie Clark. Thanks.

To Our Readers:

We have been delighted with your enthusiastic response to Candlelight Ecstasy Romances®, and we thank you for the interest you have shown in this exciting series.

In the upcoming months we will continue to present the distinctive sensuous love stories you have come to expect only from Ecstasy. We look forward to bringing you many more books from your favorite authors and also the very finest work from new authors of contemporary romantic fiction.

As always, we are striving to present the unique, absorbing love stories that you enjoy most—books that are more than ordinary romance. Your suggestions and comments are always welcome. Please write to us at the address below.

Sincerely,

The Editors
Candlelight Romances
1 Dag Hammarskjold Plaza
New York, New York 10017

DESTINY'S LADY

CHAPTER ONE

"Not even your own mother would recognize you."

"I can believe that. I don't even recognize myself." Cindy Carroll stared at her face in the mirror, a face that had undergone many changes over the past twenty-four years but none as drastic as when it belonged to Madame Destiny.

"I don't think your skin is quite pale enough yet. Let me put on another layer of pancake makeup," Kay said, after studying Cindy critically.

"You've got to be kidding! I'm already as white as a ghost."

"I can't seem to get it the same shade it was the last time I put on Madame Destiny's makeup. You've been out in the sun too much lately," she accused disapprovingly. "I've warned you what your skin is going to look like when you're forty if you don't start wearing sunscreen."

"It's bound to look better than it does right now. I feel like my face is about to crack," Cindy said, stretching her mouth wide and wrinkling her nose to see what effect the movement would have on Kay's hard work. In spite of her teasing she was grateful for her friend's help. Without Kay's expertise in applying stage makeup for the local repertory theater group, Cindy's transformation from petite, ordinary assistant personnel director to the dramatic, exciting fortune-teller, Madame Destiny, would have been almost impossible.

"Be still," Kay scolded, pushing the mirror aside as she applied more base and then added a deep burgundy blush across Cindy's cheeks. "Just a dash more eye shadow and a final adjustment to your wig and we'll be ready to go. We wouldn't want Madame Destiny to be late."

"Madame Destiny wishes she didn't have to show up at all," Cindy commented, the rapid drumming of her red, inch-long, artificial fingernails revealing her nervousness. "I can't remember how I got talked into this weird masquerade in the first place, or even which brilliant mind in the charity organization came up with it, although I suspect it was Preston Pearson in both cases."

"I suspect you might be right about good old Preston, but you have to admit that every time you show up at a charity function dressed as Madame Destiny, you always attract quite a crowd—a paying crowd that brings a lot of money into the charity's coffers." Kay ran a comb through the glossy black wig. Parted in the middle, it hung thickly over Cindy's shoulders and down her back, completely covering her own short strawberry-blond hair. "You really shouldn't worry so much about these events. So far you've done great, or rather Madame Destiny has. She has an accuracy rate that any fortune-teller would envy."

"Jean Dixon has nothing to fear from me. I wouldn't do this unless it were for charity. I'd feel guilty taking people's money if I didn't know it was all going for a good cause." Cindy blotted her lips on a tissue. "Most of my predictions are so vague, they could apply to anyone, unless I've met the person and can add a little spice that I already know about them."

"I don't think it's what you say but how you say it. I never realized you were such a good actress. I wish I could talk you into trying out for a part in one of our plays. Once you put on this outfit and sit behind a crystal ball, you *become* Madame Destiny. You're really convincing, Cindy. Remember how you charmed those teenagers at the orphanage last month?"

"Oh, but that was easy. I remember from my own teenage years that the only things important to me were boys, clothes, boys, dancing and listening to the radio, boys, movies, boys, my grades, boys, having enough money, and, of course, boys. All I had to do was tell them that they could overcome the rough breaks in their lives and be as happy and successful as they wanted to be.

"Those girls really touched me," she continued, a faint frown wrinkling her forehead. "I can't believe there are so many children caught in the system who want nothing more than to be loved and accepted. I wanted to take them all home with me, but this apartment is hardly big enough for the two of us, much less twenty-six more females. Imagine how impossible it would be to get into the bathroom."

Kay chuckled at the idea but spoke seriously. "I know what you mean. Being a teenager is bad enough, but it must be even worse to have to go through those years without at least one parent. But that wasn't your only success. Don't forget how well Madame Destiny performed at the retirement home."

"Oh, don't remind me about that one. After I got there and looked at all those expectant faces filled with character and experience, I was terrified. What could I possibly tell these nice old people about their lives that they didn't already know? I could just see myself reading their palms and repeating over and over, 'Wow! Just look at that life line!' " Cindy rolled her eyes at the memory.

"But everything turned out okay."

"We all had a great time after I realized those people didn't care what I said. They were so excited to have someone pay them a little attention and add something different to their days that they didn't care who I was. After I noticed that they wanted to do most of the talking, things went pretty smoothly."

"Then why are you so nervous about tonight? You've done this at least half a dozen times, so why is this one different?" her friend asked.

"I'm not sure. I think it might be because of that memo my new boss sent to all the employees at the company. He didn't come right out and order everyone to show up, but he did encourage participation in rather forceful words. I guess I'm afraid I'll make a fool of myself in front of my associates."

"Don't be ridiculous. Most of those people would admire your dedication and the time you spend with a charitable organization," Kay said, scoffingly, trying to offer a boost of encouragement. "Besides, like I said before, the chance that someone would recognize you is practically nonexistent. Other than the unseen flesh and blood, you and Madame Destiny have almost nothing in common."

"I don't know whether that's an insult or a compli-

14

ment," Cindy responded with an amused smile as she stood up and stepped into the black spike-heeled shoes that added three inches to her diminutive height. She crossed the room to the closet door so she could check out her appearance in the full-length mirror.

Madame Destiny always wore the same costume, but each time she looked at herself after Kay had worked her magic, Cindy couldn't believe the incredible difference.

"With all the makeup, this wig, and the skintight black dress, I can never decide whether I look more like Morticia from *The Addams Family* or that woman called Elvira who hosts those trashy old horror movies on Saturday nights. Of course, I don't have as much cleavage as Elvira," Cindy added in mild dismay.

"Few women do." Kay shrugged. "If you're really worried about it, though, we could always add a little padding—"

"No way," Cindy quickly objected. "I'm already wearing tinted contacts to make my eyes look dark brown, fake fingernails, a mile of phony hair, ten pounds of makeup, and a dress that looks like it's been painted on my body. I think those are as many artificial additions as a person can bear."

"It was just a suggestion. You don't really need it, anyway. Your figure may not knock a guy's eyes out, but you fill out that dress very nicely."

"Thanks, Kay. You did a great job. Now, if only Madame Destiny can live up to her reputation tonight and keep her imagination and ability to ad-lib. Well, let's go and get it over with."

As Kay flipped off the other lights in the small apartment, Cindy picked up her purse and gauzy black lace veil that she could use to further conceal her identity. She was determined to do everything in her power not to be recognized tonight. Taking a deep, shaky breath, Cindy Carroll walked through her apartment doorway, leaving behind her everyday personality. The mysterious, all-knowing, intriguing Madame Destiny had begun to take over.

By the time they arrived at the huge concrete parking lot next to the high school football stadium where the fund-raiser was being held, the veil was pinned firmly in place and the caterpillar had completed her transformation into an exotic butterfly. Even her voice had lost its soft Virginia drawl as she lowered it an octave and took on a foreign accent of questionable origin. Never particularly talented with language studies in school, Cindy always practiced for days before an appearance, being careful not to be overheard by anyone other than her roommate.

"I think I sound more like Catherine Deneuve every moment, don't you, *mon ami?*" she asked in her best husky French voice.

Kay, who had an excellent ear for accents, tried to hide a smile. "You're my dearest friend and I wouldn't hurt your feelings for the world, but Catherine Deneuve has never sounded like that. Actually your accent is more like Zsa Zsa Gabor with occasional lapses into Pepe LePew."

"I'm crushed! You're telling me I sound like a cross between a Hungarian and a cartoon skunk?"

"At least he's French."

"Small consolation."

But Cindy took the teasing in the spirit in which it

16

was intended. She knew Kay was just trying to help her relax by keeping the conversation light.

It was still early, and only the cars of the other volunteer workers were clustered together in the vast lot. Kay dropped her off and promised she would come back later to browse and spend money like everyone else. From now to the end of Madame Destiny's tour of duty tonight, they couldn't be seen together or someone might figure out Cindy's true identity. Madame Destiny was on her own.

A large part of the parking lot had been decorated to look like a carnival midway. Food and game booths had been arranged to form several rows. At the very back of the area a platform had been set up from which an eclectic collection of donated items would be auctioned later in the evening. Strings of light bulbs had been stretched back and forth overhead to provide a bright, cheerful atmosphere even after dark. Lots of colorful balloons with the charity's logo printed on them not only added to the overall spirit of the event but also offered a gentle reminder of why everyone was there.

Cindy's restless gaze took it all in as she searched for that one special booth that would be hers for the next few hours. At last she saw it, nestled cozily in a position of honor between the Wheel of Chance booth and the hot dog vendor, two of the most popular stops at any carnival. The walls were draped in a shiny black-and-red-striped material, then rose to a point, making her booth look like an Arabian tent. A large gold sign painted with bold black letters announcing simply MADAME DESTINY—FORTUNE-TELLER was hung over the doorway, and a small table had been set up in front of the tent where tickets would be sold.

17

"Oh, Madame Destiny, it's so good to have you here with us again," a plump, middle-aged woman dressed as a gypsy exclaimed, rushing toward Cindy. "Doesn't it all look magnificent? And the weather is just perfect. We're expecting quite a crowd tonight, so I hope your crystal ball is all shined and ready to go."

"But of course," Cindy answered in character. "It is right here in my bag."

"My name is Gloria Hopper, and I'll be sitting right out here if you need anything. I'm sure we'll be the busiest booth in the place. I'll collect the money, then send them in to see you. If you need to take a break, just let me know and I'll arrange it with the people waiting."

"Thank you."

"It's almost six o'clock. They'll be opening the gates soon."

Cindy nodded and walked through the curtain of tinkling scarlet beads to the inner sanctum. It took her a few minutes to light and arrange the candles to create the proper atmosphere. She was particularly careful to make certain her client's faces would be partially lit while her own remained obscured by shadows. Then she adjusted the spotlight so it would focus a concentrated beam of light on the area she wanted her clients to pay attention to: the small, round table and the sparkling crystal ball on its center.

Satisfied at last that everything looked properly mysterious, Cindy told Gloria that she was ready for the first customer, then sat back to wait. Her nervousness returned in a wave of panic. A tremor shook her body as if she had a chill. Something was going to happen tonight, she was certain of it. She didn't know what, but

18

she knew that it would be something strange and exciting, maybe even a little wild.

Perhaps she was just a bit psychic, after all, she told herself with a weak chuckle.

The beads rattled, and a woman hesitantly entered the tent. Her eyes blinked rapidly as she adjusted to the almost total darkness.

"Be seated," Madame Destiny's husky voice demanded, and the woman obeyed. Cindy breathed a sigh of relief. She recognized the woman as a new employee at her company. That would make this job a lot easier.

"Welcome to the tent of Madame Destiny. Would you prefer that I first read your palm to tell you about your life, or see what the crystal ball says about your future?" she asked in her best accent.

"The crystal ball, please," the woman whispered hoarsely. Cindy wondered if her first customer was even more nervous than Madame Destiny.

"Hmm," she murmured, her hands moving in graceful circles over the crystal ball. Her vivid red fingernails looked startling in the artificial lighting. "Aha!" she said, as if the image within the ball had suddenly become clear. Fanning her fingers around its base, she peered into its depths as she considered what she should say.

Because she worked in the personnel department, she had access to everyone's personnel files. She didn't snoop through them, but one of the duties of her job was to go over each application. Then, after a person was hired, she had to check to see that all the necessary forms were completed and included in the individual's file. Through the course of handling all this paperwork she absorbed many of the details, both professional and personal. These very details could prove very useful to-night if many of Wainwright Ink's employees showed up and wanted their fortunes told. But she had to be extremely selective on what she chose to use.

Definitely nothing too personal or embarrassing, she decided. And nothing that these same people wouldn't freely tell someone else in the course of a normal conversation. It was a touchy situation and she would have to handle it carefully.

But she had also done her homework on the mechanics of fortune-telling and palm reading. After studying several books on the subjects Cindy felt she was knowledgeable enough to give a fairly accurate reading of the lines and mounts of any hand. Oddly enough, it was amazing how closely nature's markings matched her own knowledge about each person. Although she couldn't believe it as absolute truth, she couldn't completely discount it, either.

And, of course, the crystal ball revealed nothing more to her than it did to anyone else. This was the part of the fortune-telling session where she tried to give sensible and harmless advice to people. She told them only good, positive things that were usually generalized, and she always avoided business or marital advice that could make her customer do something drastic. But by carefully watching her client's reactions and listening to his or her comments, she could revise the subjects and suggestions to those she felt they wanted to hear.

"I see that you have recently made a big change in your life . . . a new job, perhaps. It is a good company. You will do well there, moving up to a permanent position soon." She continued to boost the woman's obviously low confidence and commented on her children and husband. The woman left several minutes later, smiling happily and feeling very satisfied with what she had been told.

Cindy continued for the next two hours, passing on her knowledge and predictions to a steady stream of people. Some of them were acquaintances, but many she had never met before. As the evening progressed, her confidence grew with every new customer who passed through her beaded curtain. As she listened to their murmurs of approval or gasps of astonishment when she told them some little-known truth, she fell deeper and deeper into her role. Soon shy little Cindy had been completely taken over by her more spectacular counterpart. Her gestures became increasingly dramatic and her accent even more outrageous. Once she relaxed, she actually began to enjoy herself.

But even psychics needed nourishment, and the inviting odors from the hot dog stand next door were driving her wild. Since it wouldn't be proper for Madame Destiny's stomach to add comments to her fortune-telling monologue, she decided she deserved a break. After Gloria returned with a chili dog Cindy discovered that it was more difficult than she had imagined to try to eat with a veil. She finally gave up, pushing the lacy scarf on top of her head long enough to eat. There wasn't anyone waiting in line, so she felt relatively safe as she enjoyed her dinner. She had barely finished with the last bite and was trying to check the awkwardly long fingernails for signs of mustard when she heard voices outside her tent.

"Oh, come on, Nicky. You *must* have your fortune told. I need to know what your plans for the future are," a feminine voice said, drifting through the thin barrier of material.

"Don't worry, Felicia. You'll be the first person to know," a deep masculine voice replied.

"But I want to know now. Please. Do it for me," she urged.

"You know I hate this sort of thing," the man said, protesting in a loud whisper. "This fortune-telling stuff is a lot of baloney."

"No, it's not. I had my palm read by this very same person, and she told me the man I would marry would be very rich and drive a sports car . . . and that fits you perfectly, Nicky."

"There are lots of rich men who drive sports cars," the man replied, scoffing.

"Not in Petersburg, Virginia, darling."

Cindy was shamelessly eavesdropping by then. She thought she recognized the man's voice and found herself holding her breath as she waited for his next words. She didn't remember her session with the woman, but it wasn't difficult to put together a mental picture of what she looked like. She probably would be slim and immaculately dressed and definitely very beautiful. In fact, she was probably everything Cindy was not.

"Honey, it would only take a few minutes of your time, and it would make me very happy to know that you did it just for me," the woman continued, the pout as obvious in her speech as it probably was on her mouth.

"Good Lord, Felicia." He snorted, sounding tired of the whole conversation.

"Please?"

"This is so stupid," he grumbled, but Cindy could tell

22

by the sounds of movement outside that he was heading toward the entrance. "I want you to remember that I'm only doing this because for some unknown reason it seems to mean so much to you."

"Oh, yes. It does. But you have to promise to tell me everything she says, especially if it concerns me."

"I'm sure everything she says will be so general and vague that it could concern anyone," the man muttered, obviously not caring whether or not anyone, including Madame Destiny, heard him.

At the last possible second Cindy remembered to lower her veil as the clicking of the beads announced the man's entrance. Having to duck his head to clear the almost six-foot-high opening, he paused, as everyone inevitably did, trying to separate the image of Madame Destiny from the darkness. His broad shoulders filled the doorway as the lights behind him silhouetted what appeared to be a well-developed male physique. Cindy's voice caught in her throat as he stepped farther into the tent. He didn't wait for her invitation to sit down but moved purposefully across the small space and made himself as comfortable as possible on the folding chair, unknowingly giving her an excellent view of his face.

It really was him . . . the same Nicholas Wainwright Cindy had had a painful crush on in high school. Of course, since he had been a senior and she had been a practically invisible freshman, he had never known she existed. But she had never forgotten him.

Other men had come and gone in her life, but through the years newspaper articles and casual comments by mutual friends had kept thoughts of Nick in her mind. She had heard of his adventures as he went through college, and later, as he bounced from job to job before finally returning to Petersburg and taking over his father's business, the same company at which Cindy had been employed since her graduation from business school. The man who had sent her innocent teenage libido into such a frenzy was now her boss, and the passing years had done nothing to lessen his appeal in her eyes.

But their offices were on opposite sides of the building and he had only been back for six months, so she hadn't seen much of him except at a few crowded meetings. And, unfortunately, history had repeated itself and he still didn't know she existed.

Nick shifted in his chair and cleared his throat, trying to get some response from the woman sitting across from him. All he wanted was for her to hurry and get this thing over with so he and Felicia could finish making the rounds of the booths before the auction started. There was a great-looking antique jukebox he would love to buy, and he didn't want to miss out on it.

Cindy saw his impatience and struggled to collect her thoughts. This was no ordinary customer, and she was having trouble making her brain work. Taking a deep breath, which she hoped would regulate the skipping beat of her heart, she gave him her standard opening speech, exaggerating her accent even more than usual.

"Welcome to the tent of Madame Destiny. Would you prefer that I first read your palm to tell you about your life, or see what the crystal ball says about your future?"

"Look, I don't mean to be rude, but I think I can save us both a lot of time," he said, his tone revealing his indifference. Giving her an indulgent half smile to soften his words, he continued, "You might say that I'm

24

extremely skeptical of all this." His nod toward the crystal ball also included her. "I realize that you're just doing this for charity, so I can't really censure it. As long as you understand that I know this is a harmless little game and that I don't believe you or anyone else has the power to tell my future."

She couldn't really be angry at his attitude, because she had no misconceptions about her powers. But she did know how to read palms, and she knew a lot more about Nicholas Wainwright than he would ever guess. All those days of watching him with adoring eyes as he threw a winning touchdown at a high school football game or made witty, slightly embarrassed speeches as he accepted yet another award given him by classmates or coaches would come in handy. Then there were all those newspaper clippings that had followed his less-than-illustrious college years, not to mention the remarks she had overheard that were made by his alternately proud and exasperated father.

Stiffening her back and lifting her chin regally, Cindy vowed to give him the best darn reading of her career. She would amaze Nick Wainwright with her intuitiveness and wow him with her accuracy. He would leave the tent wondering whether he possibly could have misjudged her. But she knew she would have to work for it.

"Many have entered this room as skeptics and left as believers," she stated grandly. "Now, if you will let me look at your left hand, I will tell you things you've never known about yourself."

"Sure," he muttered, but he extended his hand toward her as she had requested.

Cindy had another moment of panic as she took his hand in hers and held it, palm up. It was the first time

25

she had actually touched him, and the warmth of his skin against hers did strange things to her equilibrium. She couldn't count all the male hands she had held, both in the line of charity work and for more personal reasons. But, as silly as it seemed, the weight and feel of his hand in hers caused all those wonderfully innocent teenage dreams to come flooding back.

How many times had she wished he would notice her and recognize all the wonderful qualities she had hidden beneath her rather ordinary exterior? She had dreamed of that instant when their eyes would meet and he would be captivated by what he saw. Of course, then he would ask her to go out on a date with him where they would talk and laugh and do much more than just hold hands.

But it had never happened, and now, even though their hands were together, it couldn't have been less personal—for him, anyway. It was a moment she would remember always.

She mentally shook the cobwebs out of her brain as she rubbed her fingertips over his palm, lightly massaging the fleshy mounds and deeply etched lines. "I can see by your palm that you will live a long, vital life. Except for a bad accident or illness when you were younger, you are strong and should have no major health problems. I see that you have a lot of enthusiasm about things that interest you. You should be very active, even in your old age."

"Oh, come on, *Madame*," he said almost derogatorily. "Show me where you see all these things. Please excuse me if I can't quite accept all this."

"Of course, *sir*. I'd be delighted." With the scarlet tip of her index finger Cindy lightly followed the crease

26

that curved around the base of his thumb. "This is your life line. See how long and clearly marked it is? That tells me you should live to a ripe old age. And it's smooth except for this one break toward the top, which means that you should be healthy. The break shows that your life changed suddenly because of an accident or illness. Because it is located in the upper third of the line means it happened in your late teens or early twenties. Look at the way it swoops toward the bottom of your hand. That's where I can see your strength and enthusiasm."

Nick said nothing, but Cindy knew she had his complete attention. Even if she hadn't remembered hearing that he had broken his elbow in his senior year of college, ruining his chances of a promising career in professional football, it had been clearly imprinted on his palm. She went on with her reading, pointing out his head line and telling him that the way it dipped down toward the heel of his hand showed he was creative and imaginative; it's separation from the life line above his thumb told of his adventurous nature. She pointed out several tiny crisscrosses cutting the line that showed he had recently been under a great deal of mental anguish but was quick to point out that the line smoothed out after these crossings, proving that he would be able to work things out.

She knew she had him hooked after she showed him the line running down the middle of his palm, explaining that this fate line told that he had been successful in his youth, then a break in the line said he had faded slightly before changes in his career brought him a new, better, more lasting success. She told him that, according to the location of the break in the line, his renewed success should come from a venture he had started within the last few months. She went on by pointing out his fame line and his health line and telling him what their different markings meant.

He was leaning over the table by then, intently watching the movement of her long red fingernail as it tickled his palm. She knew he was listening to her, carefully comparing what she said with what he already knew.

"And this," she said, slowly and sensuously caressing the long, curved line that began between his index and second fingers, "is your heart line, which tells everything about your love life."

"I can't wait to hear this," he remarked, his tone considerably warmer and more relaxed than when he had first sat down.

Neither could Cindy. Somehow talking about this line on which she fervently wished to be included was more difficult than all the rest.

"I see that you've been busy. All these little breaks show the many different romances with which you have been involved. You've dated many women, but none of them have meant anything special to you. There is someone, however, that you will become involved with quite soon that is that one perfect mate for you. I see that you will only marry once in your life, and it will be a long and happy marriage. You have a warm, romantic nature and are capable of having a deep romantic attachment when the right woman comes along."

Turning his hand slightly so she could show him the lines on the side of his hand under his little finger, she added with a chuckle, "And I see that you and your wife will have five lovely children."

"Good Lord! Five?" he exclaimed with a genuine grin. "Show me where you see *that.*"

"Right here," she answered, pointing to the five tiny but distinct lines rising from a deep horizontal line that she identified as his marriage line..

"Five kids?" he repeated, shaking his head, not so much in disbelief but in dismay.

"I'm afraid so. A person's palm never lies about such things."

"Huh. You're better than I thought," he admitted grudgingly as she moved her hands away from his.

Flexing his fingers after the inactivity, he leaned back in the chair and looked at her sharply. It aggravated him that he couldn't see her face or make out any of her features. He didn't like talking to people if he couldn't meet their eyes. She had nice hands with slim, graceful fingers, their length exaggerated by the scarlet fingernails. He could barely make out the outline of a very nice figure emphasized by the tight black dress, and the tantalizing view of the soft skin revealed by the plunging neckline more than caught his interest. If only the lighting weren't so bad, maybe he could discover just who this Madame Destiny really was and add her to his already crowded heart line. With her husky voice, in spite of its weird accent and the shadow of mystery that surrounded her, she had captured his imagination. He knew he had taken much more of her time than he should have, but he didn't want to go yet.

"So tell me, Madame Destiny. What do you see in that crystal ball of yours about my future?"

"I thought you weren't interested in my crystal ball," she responded, pleased that he obviously was in no hurry to leave.

29

"I've changed my mind. About several things, in fact. And now I'd like to hear the rest. But forget the boring things. Just tell me about my love life. I want to hear more about that wife and those five kids."

Cindy saw the twinkle in his beautiful blue eyes, and even the semidarkness couldn't lessen the powerful impact she felt when he looked directly at her. She sensed his interest in her—or rather in Madame Destiny—but even so, it felt wonderful. If only she could get him to look at Cindy Carroll the same way. If only there were some way to make his sexy, masculine mouth curve into a smile whenever she was with him, or feel his lips caress hers, moving down until they found that sensitive spot on her neck and— Abruptly she stopped that line of thought before it got out of hand. Already she was feeling a little overheated in her costume in spite of the gentle breeze of a fan circulating the air in her small tent.

As she leaned over the crystal ball, moving her hands over it, a thought struck her. This was her one chance to catch his attention. If she let it slip by, he would go through the rest of his life never realizing there was a woman named Cindy who was absolutely crazy about him. She felt an idea begin to crystalize. But it was too risky . . . too wild . . . too farfetched. He would never believe it. But she had him convinced about her powers so far, she rationalized. If she phrased it right and didn't overplay it, perhaps it would at least plant the idea in his mind and he could take it from there.

She didn't give herself time to weigh the possible consequences. It was one of those spur-of-the-moment thoughts that came from nowhere and couldn't be restrained.

"Hmm," she began, gripping the crystal ball so tightly that her knuckles turned white. Lowering her voice to a dramatic whisper, partly to heighten the tension and partly to keep nosy ears outside the tent from overhearing, she rushed headlong into the first phase of her plan.

"I see that you are currently dating a woman . . . very pretty, very interested in money and having a good time. But you've already begun to get a little bored with her. No, I see your perfect woman as being someone entirely different . . . someone intelligent, with a sense of humor . . . someone who would be both your best friend and your lover."

"Go on," he encouraged, leaning forward and trying to see inside the ball.

"Yes, I can see her clearly now. She's not very tall or exceptionally beautiful, but she has a wonderful personality."

"I've been on blind dates with women like that, and they turned out to be real dogs," he said with a mischievous grin.

"Shh," she reprimanded. "You're breaking Madame Destiny's concentration. She's not beautiful," she repeated, choosing her words carefully, "but she is pretty. I see that she either lives or works very near you. In fact, she's been right under your nose for years, and you've never noticed her. But you should seek her out. I see the letter *W* and a roomful of machines. Does this sound familiar?"

"Yes . . . yes, it's my company, Wainwright Ink. We have a large *W* on the wall of the reception area and machinery in the warehouse where our products are manufactured and packaged," he answered with enthu-

31

siasm. "What else do you see? What color hair does she have? Can you see a name in there?" He was almost standing in his effort to see what Madame Destiny was looking at so intently. Could she really see some sort of image in that ridiculous, clear ball, or was she pulling his leg?

"Let me see that thing," he demanded, unable to keep his curiosity under control any longer.

Obligingly she tilted the crystal ball in his direction and said, "See? She's right there. She has short blondish hair. The next time you see her she will be wearing a blue dress. In fact, I can see her standing next to a little table and it looks like—this may sound very strange, but it looks like she's making a pot of coffee. There's also a soda machine in the room, a refrigerator, several larger tables, chairs, and I see a clock on the wall . . . let me see, it's not very clear, but it looks like nine-thirty. Do you see all these things?"

"No, I don't see anything except my own image . . . and it's upside down," he grumbled, a little disappointed.

"It's right there," Cindy continued innocently. "I can see it very clearly. Perhaps you're still skeptical and can't see through the mist of prejudice over your eyes. If only you could trust Madame Destiny. She is trying to lead you to the path of true love."

"This is very weird" was Nick's only response as he sat back down on the chair.

"I showed you the markings on your palm, and you must admit that I have been correct about many things so far. I am right about this too. You must keep looking for her until you find her. I promise you will not be disappointed."

32

"And when can I expect to meet this paragon of virtue?"

"Soon . . . perhaps even next week."

He sat for a few seconds longer, digesting the information. "No name?"

"No, I don't see a name, but I see that she's wearing a gold ring with a strange-colored stone on her right hand."

"Well, thanks, Madame Destiny. It's been real . . . interesting." He stood up and began walking toward the door, stopping just inside the entrance. "I'll let you know if I do meet this woman. Is there somewhere I can reach you if I have any more questions?"

"Madame Destiny donates all her talents to charity. Perhaps at another charity event our paths will cross."

"By then I'll probably be married to the blond woman in blue," he said jokingly.

"Don't forget the five children," she reminded him with a smile in her voice.

"At least she knows how to make coffee." He laughed, tossing the amazing Madame Destiny a jaunty wave before he ducked through the opening in the tent.

CHAPTER TWO

"You told him what?"

Kay and Cindy were back in their apartment, relaxing and talking about the fund-raiser. Kay was sitting on her bed, propped against the headboard by a cushion of pillows, while Cindy slouched in an armchair, resting her feet on the end of the bed. Dressed in a shortie gown, she had completely discarded all vestiges of her costume except for the fingernails, which she was removing as she told Kay about her meeting with Nick.

"I believe I said that he would not be disappointed when he found this perfect woman."

"Meaning you?"

"It seemed like a good idea at the time." Cindy managed a shaky smile as she tried to justify her rash actions.

"Do you know what that sounds like you're promising him?"

"I didn't mean it *that* way. I just meant that I believed he and this woman would have something special together."

Kay shook her head in disbelief. "But Nick Wainwright of all people. Why did you choose him to drop this bombshell on? I didn't even realize he was back in town."

"I told you a few months ago that after Mr. Wainwright died, his son took over the company. He's my new boss," Cindy explained as she pretended to concentrate on prying off one fingernail.

"I thought you meant his younger brother, Rory. I never dreamed that Nick would settle down long enough to do something as sedate as watching people make ballpoint pens."

"Rory is still in graduate school and didn't feel he was ready to take over such a huge responsibility. Besides, I think Nick will be a wonderful boss," Cindy said, defending him. "He's very intelligent, friendly, and caring. When he had that accident, he was very disappointed about not being able to go on to play professional football. He had been working so hard toward that goal that when the chance of success was taken away, he was at loose ends. I guess he's been trying to find something else to do with his life, experimenting with different jobs—"

"And different women."

"Maybe." She shrugged, not wanting to think about that particular part of Nick's life. "To some people that may look like he's a little undependable, but now that he's moved back and focused his life, he'll settle down quickly."

"But why . . ." Kay stared at her friend as it suddenly dawned on her that Cindy's motivation might have been more than playfulness. "You couldn't possibly still have a crush on that man, could you?"

"Well, I think *crush* is sort of a juvenile word, but if

you mean am I still attracted to him, yes, I am," Cindy admitted as a pink flush colored her cheeks.

"But we haven't seen him since he graduated from high school and went to college somewhere. I thought you forgot about him years ago. I certainly had."

Cindy was silent for a few moments as she considered how to explain her feelings for Nick without making it sound like she had some sort of weird obsession. "Hasn't there ever been that one special man in your life that made your knees weak every time you saw him and the thought of him holding you and kissing you sent shivers through your body?"

At Kay's reluctant nod Cindy went on, "Well, that's the way it's always been with Nick for me. On those lonely Saturday nights when I didn't have a date in high school, I drooled over his picture in the annual until the book opened to that page automatically. He was always so popular and at the time seemed so much older and more mature that I knew I never had a chance with him. But I never missed a football game when he was the quarterback or an assembly when he made a speech."

"I never realized you had it that bad for him," Kay commented sympathetically. "But you've dated other guys that I thought you were serious about."

"I tried not to think about him because I figured it was hopeless. But none of those other guys ever gave me that special feeling. Oh, some of them were very nice and I've probably been wasting my life wishing for something I can't have. But it's not like I'm so fixated that I couldn't fall in love with someone else. It's just that he's always been the ideal against whom all the

36

other men I've met have been measured. It's not my fault that none of them have ever come close."

"I hope your adolescent idolatry hasn't blown his memory all out of proportion. He's just a man, not a god."

"I know that. But it seemed like the chance of a lifetime for me to find out the truth. Maybe once I see that he's not as perfect as I've always thought, I'll be able to stop being so critical about other men."

"So now you've gotten him interested in this mystery woman." Kay voiced the question that was foremost in both of their minds. "What are you going to do with him if he's waiting in the coffee room next week?"

Cindy looked a little panicky. She had begun to wonder that very same thing, and the prospect frightened her. "I'm not sure," she finally admitted. "I didn't think that far ahead. I could only think about what I should do to make him notice me. It didn't occur to me that once he did notice me, I might have to carry on a conversation with him. If I were dressed up like Madame Destiny, I could handle it. She's much bolder and more confident that I."

"But she *is* you," Kay offered reassuringly. "And if Nicholas Wainwright is the man that makes your blood race, then I say go for it. You might find out that you've been waiting all these years for a dud. So what if he was the most gorgeous man to graduate from Petersburg High? He might be a real creep once you get to know him better."

"It doesn't matter, anyway." Cindy exhaled, releasing a deep sigh. "I probably won't have enough nerve even to go near that coffee room next week. Even if I did and he showed up, after spending a few seconds

37

with me he'll think Madame Destiny needs glasses to see the image in the crystal ball more clearly."

But on Monday morning at nine-twenty Cindy, dressed in a slinky teal-blue dress that was almost too fancy for wearing to the office, was busy measuring coffee grinds into the white filter at the top of the large aluminum pot. She had taken extra pains with her short, strawberry-blond hair, coaxing some curl into the jaw-length style until it feathered back from her face. Her naturally dark eyelashes had been thickened with a coat of mascara to highlight her large hazel eyes, and a light touch of blusher added extra color to her early tan. She felt she looked the very best she possibly could and wished that Nick would hurry up and put in an appearance before she chewed off her lipstick.

By nine-fifty she had not only finished with the coffee but also had cleaned out the refrigerator. Still there was no sign of the man. Obviously neither his thirst nor his curiosity was going to bring him to the coffee room. The only reasonable thing for her to do was swallow her disappointment and return to her desk, hoping that her lengthy absence hadn't been too noticeable.

Tuesday morning at nine twenty-five she was back in the coffee room, struggling to rinse out the heavy pot and fill it with fresh water. She was careful not to splash any on her blue jersey dress as she carried the pot back to the table and fitted a filter into the basket. It had been a little humid that morning and her hair didn't have as much curl as it had the day before, but it still looked good enough to satisfy her critical eyes.

By nine forty-five she had washed all the dirty cups and straightened the cabinets over the sink. The only person who had come to refill his cup of coffee had been

38

one of the salesmen who had shown his approval of the way she looked by asking her to go dancing with him that night. It took him several minutes to take no for an answer as he practiced his best self-promotional line on her.

If only Nick could be as attentive and interested in her as this unwelcome suitor, Cindy thought. Why couldn't she feel the same attraction for another man that she felt for Nick? Cindy was disappointed and more than a little bit discouraged as she returned to her desk and quickly buried herself in her work.

When he didn't show up on Wednesday, Cindy knew it was time to accept defeat. Apparently he either hadn't believed Madame Destiny or, worse, was just not interested in meeting a woman matching Cindy's description. She absently filled her coffee cup with the freshly perked brew and tried to blame the hollow feeling in the pit of her stomach on all the coffee she had been drinking lately. What was she doing, anyway, cleaning the refrigerator and cabinets, washing the cups, making a list of needed supplies, and manhandling that heavy pot back and forth from the sink? She hadn't done that much housework in her own apartment lately.

It was time to face facts. Nick wasn't going to show up at nine-thirty on *any* morning. She was not only wasting her time but also she was making a fool of herself. Madame Destiny had gotten her into this, giving her delusions of grandeur. Well, she had to be more realistic. The only intelligent thing to do would be to stop thinking of Nick as anything other than what he was: her boss.

She reached into the pocket of her royal-blue shirt-waist and took out some change. Going to the snack machine, she put her money in the slot and pulled the handle beneath the coffee cakes. She might as well take something back to her desk to eat with her half full cup of coffee. With a sigh she resolved that this would be the last morning she would be there waiting like an anxious old maid. She may not be beautiful or blatantly sexy, but she had enough going for her that she didn't have to degrade herself another day.

Besides, she had run out of blue dresses.

Thursday morning Don, the personnel director, was out of town, which left Cindy in charge. By nine o'clock she had already conducted two interviews and answered what seemed like a thousand telephone calls.

Cindy really loved her job at Wainwright Ink. After finishing two years of business school and earning her associate's degree, she had marched boldly but innocently into the job market, totally unprepared for the rejections she soon received. Her skills were excellent, her grades had been at the top of her class, but she was hampered by having absolutely no business experience.

Only Nick's father had been willing to take a chance on an eager but untried young woman. Hired as an entry-level secretary in the pool, she had soon worked her way up to the personnel department. When the personnel director had retired, Don had moved up, taking Cindy with him as his assistant. He was a good supervisor, always expecting a little more out of her than she realized she had to give, and always getting it. But Don had had an emergency with his wife's parents and had to fly to Florida to be with them. To make things worse, their secretary was out sick, which left Cindy alone to handle both the phones and the inter-office work.

Between calls she was trying to put the new employ-

40

ees' files into the computer so the payroll department could print out the checks in time for payday on Friday. She would type in a couple of lines of information at a time, answer a call, then find the place where she had left off and try to type in a few more lines before being interrupted again. By nine-thirty her concentration was fading and her nerves were beginning to fray. Reaching for her coffee cup, she decided to take a very necessary break and left word with the receptionist to hold the calls.

A group of men from the factory were just leaving the coffee room as she entered it. She knew them all by name and returned their friendly greetings as they passed. But when she pressed down the lever of the coffeepot and only a few thick black drops oozed out, her pleasant feelings turned to disgust.

"Why do men think they don't have to refill the pot when it's empty?" she grumbled aloud, even though there was no one else in the room to hear her. The bulky pot seemed to get heavier each day. It was ironic, she thought, that she had voluntarily made the coffee for three days in a row, and then the one day she hadn't planned on doing it, here she was, making it again. Well, she had taken her turn for the rest of the month. "If those lazy men want to drink coffee from now on, they can make it themselves," she said with a snort. "This is the eighties. It was never written that coffee making is solely a feminine job."

"I agree completely," a familiar masculine voice said so closely behind her that she almost dropped the half filled pot. "Here, let me do that."

She didn't have to turn around to know it was Nick. All she could think of was that he had come—three

41

days late—but then, Madame Destiny hadn't been specific on the date. The important thing was that he was in the same room talking to her. But, darn it, why did he have to catch her in such an awkward position, struggling to hold the coffeepot under the faucet, her hair falling forward across her face and her skirt hiked up to her thighs?

"No, I'm almost through," she answered in a small voice, wondering how much of her muttered complaints he had overheard.

"I insist," he said, reaching around her to take the pot.

He was so close, she could smell his tangy aftershave. Never in all her life had so little distance separated her from the man of her dreams. The heat of his body as it brushed against her sent unexpected waves of delight shooting through her limbs, leaving them weak. Her hands slipped from the handles quicker than he had anticipated, and the pot tipped toward them.

"Watch out!" he called.

Simultaneously she cried, "Oh, no!"

A wave of cold water sloshed out, drenching both of them. Horrified, she looked down at the dark water spot on the right side of the blue dress she had borrowed from Kay. Then her gaze moved on to the large discolored area that was in a most embarrassing place on the front of his light tan slacks.

"I'm sorry—"

"It was all my fault—"

They both began to speak at once, then stopped, waiting for the other to finish. Cindy turned her head to look up into his face, expecting to see anger but sur-

42

prised to see a sheepish smile and the most breathtaking pair of twinkling blue eyes.

"I shouldn't have been so pushy. But I guess it was the Mr. Macho in me that wanted to help out such a pretty little lady like you," he offered as an apology.

"It was just that you startled me so," she replied in her soft Virginia drawl. "I'm afraid you got more than you bargained for." She nodded toward his wet pants.

"It's been a slow morning, but that certainly woke me up." He chuckled. "I'm afraid we're both going to have to hide out for a while before returning to our offices or expect to get some strange looks."

Cindy couldn't believe how well he was taking the whole situation. She wouldn't have minded spending the rest of the day in the circle of his arms. But he was still holding the handles of the coffeepot, and she was having trouble breathing, so she ducked under his arm and backed away. He finished filling the pot, carried it over to the table, then returned to the sink and began to clean up the mess. Cindy tried to concentrate on counting the scoops of coffee she was dumping into the filter, but her attention kept wandering to the man who was squatting down to mop the water off the floor with paper towels.

The light had been too poor in Madame Destiny's tent for her to see how much more handsome he had become. The years had been good to him, taking away the boyish slimness and giving a new strength and sturdiness to his well-developed body. She had always thought he looked fantastic in his football uniform, but maturity had added even more breadth to his shoulders and depth to his chest. And she couldn't help but notice the way his athletic thigh muscles bulged against the thin material of his slacks as he balanced in the awkward position.

A thick lock of dark brown fell over his forehead as he bent over his task, and Cindy's hands ached to reach out and feel its softness beneath her fingers. She swallowed back the uncharacteristic surge of desire flashing through her and turned her back to him so she could finish making coffee without doing anything else stupid. Impatiently she pushed her own hair away from her face and wished she had taken more time with her appearance that morning. She hadn't planned on being in this room with him, and it had only been a last-minute impulse that had made her borrow the blue dress from Kay.

Finally she plugged the cord into the back of the pot and put the can of coffee on the shelf under the table. Nick had just thrown the wet paper towels in the garbage can and had taken a few dry ones to help dry the front of his pants. Taking a cue from his casualness, she tore off a few towels and attempted to blot her skirt dry.

"I assume you work here," he commented, glancing at her. "Surely you wouldn't just stop by to check on the coffee?"

Melting even more beneath the warmth of his grin, she felt herself begin to relax as her lips automatically curved into a smile. He could have made this a very humiliating encounter, but instead he was actually joking about it.

"I'm the assistant personnel director," she answered, shyly lifting her eyes to meet his crystal-blue ones.

"Then you probably already know my name. But in case you don't, I'm Nick. And you're . . . ?"

"The name on the paycheck you sign every week is Cynthia Carroll, but my friends call me Cindy."

"Cindy," he repeated. "Let's sit down for a few minutes and wait for the coffee to perk. It will give us time to find out more about . . . um, talk about the company."

Cindy didn't even have to try to convince herself to extend her break. There wasn't much in the world that she would rather do than spend more time with Nick, listening to his deep, mellow voice and staring with what she hoped wasn't obvious adoration at his fascinating face. Quickly, before he changed his mind, she sat in the chair he held out for her and watched as he settled into a chair opposite her.

Crossing his arms on the table in front of him, he leaned forward, noting the variety of emotions that flickered across her expressive face as he spoke. "I apologize for having to ask. As one of the owners of this company, I should know everyone's name, but it takes time. I've been making visits to the various departments, trying to get acquainted with all my employees, but with over three hundred permanent workers and all of the sales representatives and distribution people, I just haven't gotten around to everyone yet. I have so much to learn about the general operations that I haven't had time to become involved with the administrative part of the business. Luckily I seem to have some very competent employees handling those departments, so I don't have to worry about them right now. My dad certainly had everything under control when he . . ." His voice trailed off as his gaze wandered to some point on the wall above her shoulder.

She saw that he was having trouble keeping his feelings under control. He had obviously cared a great deal for his father, whose unexpected death had been a shock to everyone. Not to mention that it had thrust Nick into a position of responsibility where hundreds of people depended on his judgment and leadership.

"Didn't you want to get into your father's business?" she couldn't help asking.

"Oh, sure. I always knew I would come home some-day and go in with Dad," he answered slowly and thoughtfully. "But I had big plans to get rich and fa-mous in professional sports first. I thought this com-pany and my family would always be here for me if all the fun went out of the game or I got too old to play. But things don't always work out like we plan, do they?" he asked, not expecting an answer. "When an accident ended my athletic career, I wasn't ready to come back and sit in an office next to Dad's, to be a figurehead vice-president while he handled all the work."

He combed his fingers through his hair, temporarily leaving deep trails before the dark, shiny strands fell back together. Leaning back in his chair, he pressed the palms of his hands on the tabletop as he continued. "Dad was a very strong man, very proud that he had built this company from nothing. I knew that even though he loved my brother and me and trusted us, he would never pass on the control or responsibility as long as he was able to handle it himself. I couldn't see myself stringing paper clips together until he retired. So I decided to see if I could find something to interest me in the interim, maybe something I could turn into a business that would make my father proud of me. I had the mistaken idea that I had all the time in the world."

They were silent for a few seconds, each deep in thought with their own memories of the man who had ruled Wainwright Ink with a strong but fair hand.

"Nick, your father hired me when I was fresh out of junior college. He took me under his wing and treated me like a daughter. Through the years I got to know him pretty well, and I know that he was very proud of you. He couldn't stop talking about you and your achievements. He used to say that he was glad you were strong enough to go out on your own, not expecting him to hand you everything on a silver platter."

"He really said that?" Nick asked, the importance of knowing evident in the eagerness of his tone.

"Yes. Many times, in fact," she reassured him, automatically reaching out to cover his hand with hers in a comforting gesture.

But the instant her fingers touched his, it was like an electric shock, running out in both directions. Startled, their eyes met in silent uncertainty. Had they just imagined it or had something special just happened between them? Cindy wondered if only she had felt the magic of the moment, and if only her heart had skipped a beat.

Nick was wondering the same thing. Her fingers felt cool against the back of his hand and strangely stimulating. Smoothly he turned his hand until he held hers tenderly. Her hand felt small and fragile and fit perfectly in the protective curl of his fingers. A stone pressed against his palm, and he opened his hand slightly to study the gold ring she was wearing.

"That's an odd-colored stone. It's sort of purple, but there are highlights of green and blue and even a little red in it. What is it?" he asked curiously, moving her hand so that the artificial light was caught in the stone's facets.

"It's an alexandrite, my birthstone. I think they're pretty rare and can be very expensive here in the States. My father brought it back from a trip to South America several years ago," she explained. "It changes colors with the lighting, my clothing, even my moods."

"I don't think I've ever seen one like it before," he commented, suddenly reminded of the prediction that the woman he would meet in the coffee room would be wearing a ring with a strange-colored stone. Well, this was certainly the ring. Was this the woman?

The red light blinked on the coffeepot, indicating that it was ready. The thick, fragrant aroma would no doubt float down the hallway, announcing that there was a full pot. Soon the coffee room would be busy with people wanting a refill.

"I guess I'd better get back to my office before my secretary sends out a search party. It wouldn't be the first time I've gotten lost in the factory," Nick said softly, not ready to end the conversation but knowing they wouldn't be alone much longer.

"Yes, I've got tons of work waiting for me too," she agreed with a wistful smile, reluctantly drawing her hand away from his. "I really shouldn't have stayed this long."

"I promise not to tell your boss." His eyes twinkled as he stood up and took both of their coffee cups to the pot. He filled them, then turned toward the door and gave Cindy her mug.

"I guess I'll be seeing you around the office. I'll try to move the personnel department up on my list."

"Oh, please, don't make any official tours today. I'm

48

trying to handle it alone, and I don't want you to think I'm as inefficient as it would look," she pleaded in mock horror.

He chuckled and nodded. "I've really enjoyed talking with you, Cindy. And thanks for the coffee."

"You helped," she reminded him, savoring the smile he gave her just before he left the room. He was gorgeous. How could she ever hope to have a chance with him? She picked up a package of artificial sweetener and stirred it into her coffee. What did he think of her? Would he even remember her name after he got back to his office?

He startled her as he stuck his head back around the door. "By the way, Cindy, do you like kids?"

"Yes. Yes, I do," she said, practically stuttering.

"Hmm," he said with a thoughtful nod before disappearing again.

CHAPTER THREE

Nicholas Wainwright stood at the large picture window in his office. The company was located at the very edge of Petersburg, and the view of the Virginia countryside from his window was spectacular. The gently rolling land was covered in a fresh spring green with colorful wildflowers waving gently in the breeze.

But Nick wasn't thinking about the view. Nor was he thinking about the previous month's sales report that had been on his desk when he returned from his extended coffee break or the messages his secretary had handed him when he had passed through her outer office. Instead his mind was occupied with the interesting young lady he had just met. He also couldn't seem to forget a weird gypsy woman of indeterminable age who had made some startlingly accurate statements.

He hadn't believed a word of Madame Destiny's predictions and had even made it a point to avoid getting coffee at that time just to test them. But this morning things had been different, as if it were out of his control.

He had been at the office since seven, going over some designs for a new product, and had gone through two cups of coffee. He had skipped breakfast and it was still hours until lunch when he noticed his attention wandering and knew it was time for a break.

It was as simple as that. His cup had been empty, and he had been concentrating so deeply on his work that he hadn't realized what time it was. He hadn't intentionally chosen that particular time to go to the coffee room. But *she* had been there. Dressed in a bluish-green dress that had made her eyes a very intriguing shade of olive, she had been so busy fooling with the coffeepot that she hadn't even noticed him walk into the room. Why, that pot was almost as big as she was. No wonder she had been grumbling. A small woman like her shouldn't have to haul that heavy pot from the sink. She was right. The men should be expected to make the coffee too. After all, they probably drank most of it. He would have to put a memo out about that right away, he resolved.

He took a sip of the hot liquid in his earthenware mug and marveled at how much better this cup tasted than the two others he had made himself. Maybe he would get her to give him instructions to include in the memo before one of the men made everyone sick.

But back to Cindy. She had looks that couldn't be described as beautiful, but there was something about her that made her very attractive. Her face was adorable, with wide, innocent eyes and a turned-up nose sprinkled lightly with freckles. She was rather short, probably not more than two or three inches over five feet, and her figure was slim and compact but perfectly proportioned. It was an inadequate and overly used word, but Cindy Carroll was cute—sweetly, fascinatingly cute.

But their meeting that morning bothered him. Was it a coincidence? He leaned back on his desk, casually

51

crossing one ankle over the other as he considered the possibility. Could Cindy and Madame Destiny somehow have set this whole thing up? Could they be friends or acquaintances? Could Madame Destiny have told Cindy to show up at the proper time to meet him?

But none of those suggestions made any sense. He wasn't conceited enough to think that someone would go to all that trouble just to share a cup of coffee with him. Besides, Cindy had been honestly surprised to see him. With that open face of hers she couldn't possibly have been faking her reaction. And with all that mumbling and splashing, she hadn't been acting like a woman waiting to make a good impression. Besides, he couldn't ignore the fact that she *did* work at the company, longer than he had, actually, and certainly had as much right to use the coffee room as he did. No, it was all too farfetched. As much as he hated to admit it, Madame Destiny had been absolutely right so far.

Which left him with another problem. Exactly how should a person act when he knew he had met his perfect mate? Should he just come right out and tell her that she shouldn't fight it, that destiny meant them to be together? Or should he play it more subtly, hoping she'd realize he was the man for her? Suddenly a disturbing thought interrupted. What if she was *his* perfect mate but he wasn't *hers?* Could that be possible? Did it really matter?

This was getting more complicated by the moment, Nick thought. If only Madame Destiny were around so he could ask her these strange questions. He certainly couldn't ask anyone else without being carried away in a straitjacket.

He also wondered if he would have felt this attraction

for Cindy if he hadn't already been told that she might be his ideal woman. There was no denying that his temperature had risen several degrees when their hands had touched. Considering the women he had known and the things they had done, hand-holding was so incredibly tame that his reaction had surprised him. It had been a long time since a woman had affected him so easily and caused such turmoil in his thoughts. Had she felt it too? Nick thought he had seen a flash of desire in the depths of her wonderful green-gold eyes, but he wasn't sure.

Actually he knew very little about her, since he had done most of the talking. He had really opened up to her, spilled his guts about his father and the company, which he couldn't really understand at all, because he hadn't told another person many of the things he had told her. And he couldn't accuse her of digging into his personal life. She hadn't encouraged him or dragged it out of him. She had simply sat there, listening and understanding, offering him support when he needed it most. He had felt comfortable with her and hadn't felt pressed to be Mr. Cool all the time like he was with most of the other women he knew.

He lifted the almost empty mug to his lips and drained it. She certainly did make a good cup of coffee, he thought with a wry smile. And she liked kids too. Pensively he turned his left hand over and gazed down at the palm as if he could see the answer to all his questions in it. But all he saw were lines and creases. He would have to find out more about the lovely Cindy Carroll on his own. There were so many questions he wanted to ask her . . . and so many answers he would have to get from himself.

He couldn't rush into anything with her, assuming

she would be willing, of course, because he would have to be certain he was doing this because he wanted to, not because some crazy fortune-teller had told him he should. And then there was the company to think of. He wasn't sure about the proper way to handle an inter-office romance, especially now that he was the boss. He hadn't taken a stand on it one way or the other when it concerned the other employees, but as their leader, he had to play by a different set of rules.

Pushing away from the desk, he pulled out his chair and sat down. Maybe he was worrying about nothing. Cindy might have a steady boyfriend—or even be married, for that matter. They hadn't discussed her personal life at all. Nick frowned as he set down his empty mug with an unnecessarily hard thump. The thought that she might already have a man in her life was very disturbing.

Cindy was quite affected by the morning meeting as well. She had floated on air as she returned to her office, completely ignoring the questioning look from the receptionist as she picked up her messages and unlocked her office door. The pile of files had not magically disappeared, and the phone had resumed its incessant ringing by the time she stepped into the small room, but none of it bothered her anymore. Nothing mattered except that Nick had finally noticed her and really talked to her.

More importantly he had seemed to enjoy it, even after their rather rocky start. How could she have been so clumsy to have spilled water on his pants? But he hadn't gotten mad, and the spot had been hardly noticeable when he left the coffee room. She only hoped Kay would be as understanding. She looked down at the almost dry place on Kay's dress and fervently hoped it wouldn't leave a stain. But she would worry about that later. Right now she wanted to bask in the pleasure of the past half hour and remember every tiny detail.

The rest of the morning seemed to fly by as she dug into her work with renewed enthusiasm. It seemed like a fantastic dream come true, that maybe, just maybe, she had a chance with the man she had wanted for so long. Not that he had actually asked her out on a date or even said anything that would lead her to believe that he might. Of course, there had been that question about children that could have been brought on only by his talk with Madame Destiny. So his thoughts were obviously drifting in the right direction.

And he had held her hand. Such a small thing to bring her so much delight. It was as if she were a teenager again, experiencing the painfully wonderful feelings of first love when any little look or the most casual touch could bring ecstasy. But then, in a way he had been her first love, and no other man had ever been so special in her mind. And until she was able to vanquish the thought of him, no man ever would.

But she didn't want to forget him. She wanted to love him forever and have him love her in return. She still believed there could be fairy tales in real life. Especially with the extra boost from her alter ego, the exotic Madame Destiny, to help convince her prince that Cindy was worth a second look.

Her heart sang as her fingers flicked over the keyboard. She finished inputting the files on her computer terminal in record time. Picking the files up from her desk, she took them into Don's office to be filed in his cabinets. She was used to Don leaving them unlocked for their private access during office hours, and she hadn't thought to bring her keys with her. Backtracking to her desk to get them out of her purse, Cindy happened to glance out the open office door as she passed. The sight that met her eyes brought her abruptly back to earth.

A tall, fashionably thin beauty had her arm linked possessively through Nick's as they walked across the reception area toward the front doors of the building.

"I've reserved a table for us at the country club for lunch, darling. Daddy's going to meet us there, and if you promise to pay me a lot of extra attention tonight, I'll let the two of you talk about that silly old contract you want to negotiate with the city."

The voice was the same one Cindy had heard outside the tent the previous Saturday night. Even before Nick answered, she knew this must be Felicia. Not only was this woman even more beautiful than Cindy had imagined, but Nick looked anything but bored as he held the front door open for his companion.

"Thanks, Felicia. I can't tell you how much this contract means to me and the company. If I could get an exclusive to supply the municipal offices, it would really boost our business."

"It was nothing, honey. As long as you promise to support Daddy when he runs for reelection as mayor, I'm sure he'll be very grateful. And I'll let you show your appreciation to me later." The tilt of her head and the provocative way she let her body brush against his left no doubt about what she had in mind.

Cindy could hear the sound of his answering chuckle as the heavy glass door swung shut behind them. She couldn't tear her gaze away as they walked down the sidewalk, Nick's arm wrapped around Felicia's tiny waist, until they reached his shiny black Fiero GT. Holding the door open for her, he then strode around to the driver's side, and they roared out of the parking lot, a beautiful couple in a beautiful car.

Cindy felt like someone had punched her in the stomach. The keys forgotten, she rushed back into Don's office and shut the door behind her. Leaning against the wooden partition, her eyes felt hot and heavy with unshed tears. How quickly things could change. She felt like she was on a nightmare roller-coaster ride, one minute at the peak of excitement and anticipation and the next in the depths of despair and disappointment.

Sure, he had been friendly to her that morning in the coffee room. But he had never looked at her like he had just looked at Felicia. Cindy tried to convince herself that Nick was just pleased about the prospects of a lucrative contract with the city, but she knew she was grasping at straws. Dozens of business transactions were conducted every day, and none of them would have required Nick to put his arm around Felicia the way he had.

No, she had to face facts. Nick must care about Felicia more than Cindy had hoped. How could she possibly compete with someone who looked like that and had so much to offer Nick? All Cindy had to offer was her love, but would that be enough?

If possible, her day went downhill from there. She snagged her hose on the corner of a file drawer, and a wide run coursed up the outside of her leg. Deciding to eat her lunch at her desk rather than trying to be sociable in the lunchroom, she pulled out her brown paper bag and discovered that her orange had flattened her sandwich. But she accepted these minor inconveniences

57

with a stoic mental shrug. What was foremost in her mind was that she had run into a dead end.

Cindy had no idea where she should go from there. With a little help from a $10.98 crystal ball Nick had finally noticed her. But she obviously hadn't made much of an impression. She had given it her best shot and missed. Reliving the morning in her mind, she could think of hundreds of clever, intelligent things to say that might have helped her case. Why hadn't she flirted with him? Why couldn't she play all those coquettish games that other women seemed to enjoy?

That evening Cindy sat in the laundry room wallowing in self-pity as she listened to her and Kay's clothes running through the wash cycles. When she and Kay had moved in together, they had split up the chores so that Cindy did all the wash and Kay did all the grocery shopping. They took turns cooking, and each was responsible for cleaning different parts of the apartment. It was a fair arrangement with which Cindy was generally pleased. But tonight it seemed to magnify her problem. She looked on this as just one more piece of evidence that everything was wrong with her life.

Where was all the excitement? Why couldn't Nick feel the way she felt for him? It would be so much more fun to spend her evenings with him rather than a box of laundry detergent. But Nick preferred beautiful, sophisticated women, women who had probably never folded a towel in their lives, women who were better at other things. Cindy's imagination ran wild as she thought about where Nick and Felicia might be and what they were probably doing. It certainly wouldn't be waiting for the timer to go off so they could add fabric softener.

* * *

"What's the matter Nicky?" Felicia asked, trailing the edge of her fingernail through his hair. "You just haven't been yourself tonight. Didn't you and Daddy work out that contract today?"

"I'm sorry, Felicia," Nick answered, pulling away from her wandering fingers and rising from the sofa to put a little distance between them. He knew they shouldn't have come to her apartment after their date. He needed time to think, but it was obvious that Felicia had something much more active in mind. "Everything seems to be going fine with the contract. Your father is a good businessman, but I think we can reach an agreement."

"Daddy likes you a lot, you know. I think he's hoping you'll make a more permanent commitment to our family," she said, leaning back against the cushions in what she hoped would be an irresistible pose. "I don't think you'd be disappointed in what we have to offer . . . both professionally and personally."

There was that phrase again. There sure had been a lot of women lately promising that he wouldn't be disappointed. How did they know what he wanted? How could they possibly have a clue as to what would make him happy? He was beginning to feel claustrophobic and just a little trapped, like a fox being chased by a pack of drooling hounds.

The truth about the matter was that he didn't know what he wanted himself. But the one thing he did know was that he didn't want to talk about this with Felicia right now. "I haven't been very good company tonight. I think I'd better be going," Nick stated with an apologetic shrug.

In one fluid movement she was off the sofa and in his arms. Or rather he was in hers, as she wrapped her arms around his neck and pressed her body tightly against him. "Don't leave yet, Nicky. I was hoping I could talk you into spending the night with me. You never have, you know," she murmured as she planted teasing little kisses on his neck and cheeks. "Why don't you let me make you feel better?"

"Not tonight," he answered firmly, capturing her wrists in his hands and taking a few steps backward. "I'm just not in the mood right now. I don't know what's wrong with me, but today's been sort of a strange day. I'll call you tomorrow."

"Promise?" She pouted, not making any effort to try to hide her disappointment.

"Promise," he vowed, dropping a chaste kiss on her puckered lips before slipping out the door.

On the drive home he began to question his decision. Was he crazy to turn down such an offer? He knew any number of guys who would tell him he had completely lost his mind. Felicia was a very beautiful, desirable woman. But as much as he enjoyed her company and appreciated her help, he wasn't in love with her, and as far as he could tell, he never would be.

He had tried to fall in love with her, but that special spark was missing. Perhaps he had been too calculating in his choice or maybe he had tried too hard, but it just hadn't happened, at least not for him.

When he had returned to Petersburg for his father's funeral, Felicia and her father had been there to offer their condolences. She and Nick's younger sister were very good friends, so Felicia had been at his family's house almost as much as he was. When he had needed a date to take to the company's Christmas banquet, she was the only eligible female he knew who wasn't related to him. Gradually they had drifted into a dating arrangement that had provided advantages for both of them.

He found Felicia attractive and entertaining, if a little one-track-minded. And even though he knew it wasn't important in the scheme of choosing a wife, he had to admit to deriving a certain amount of pleasure from knowing that when she was with him, they drew envious stares. There was no denying that they made a striking couple.

He had discovered that wasn't enough. Nick was rapidly approaching his twenty-ninth birthday. He was tired of wandering aimlessly through life. The company was his responsibility now, and he wanted to share that and other parts of his life with someone special. It was time to stop changing women like he changed socks and settle down. He wanted it all: a wife; a house of his own; a couple of dogs; and children—two point three if the national average was correct, five if Madame Destiny was.

He had already begun to realize that Felicia was not the woman he had been waiting to find. And now Madame Destiny had just hurried his decision along. He felt badly about leading Felicia along for so many months, but he honestly had been trying to convince himself that they could make it together. And now that he had admitted to himself that they couldn't, he would feel guilty about anything that happened between them from now on. She deserved better than that.

Though he had her best interests in mind, Felicia wouldn't take it well, he suspected. She was a very determined woman who knew exactly what she wanted. And for whatever reason—he wasn't sure if it was his money, his status, his prospects for the future, or himself—she wanted him. They had never discussed love, and he suspected that her reasons for being seen with him were very similar to his for dating her. She, too, was ready to marry and had chosen him as the most acceptable candidate.

Very likely she wouldn't give up without a fight. She had invested six months in cultivating him, introducing him to everyone who was anyone in Petersburg society, and trying to get him involved with the politics that had gotten her father into the mayor's office. It hadn't seemed to matter to her that he wasn't the least bit interested in either society or politics but had gone along just to please her.

What he needed was a woman who would take him as he was and not try to mold him into a different lifestyle, someone with whom he could share his fears and hopes, someone who would be there when he needed her and who would need him. He wanted a wife who wouldn't demand more than he could give and who wouldn't judge him for past mistakes, an honest, unpretentious woman with whom he could be comfortable as they grew old together.

Could that woman be Cindy?

CHAPTER FOUR

Her secretary was still sick, and Don had called and told Cindy that things were worse than he had expected and he would be gone for at least another week.

Thank goodness it was Friday.

Fridays were the days she usually set aside for processing medical insurance claim forms for all of the company's employees. Cindy pulled all the paperwork out of the incoming insurance tray and flipped through them with a sigh of relief. There weren't too many, and with a minimum of interruptions she should be finished with them before lunch.

Naturally Murphy's Law came into effect, and it was mid-afternoon before she was able to close the codebook she used for completing the approval for the insurance papers. It always amazed her how many illnesses and obscure operations there were that she had never heard of before taking over this job. But as long as they were listed in the codebook and the proper bills and receipts were attached, she didn't question them. She just thanked her lucky stars that her only visits to the hospital had been when she was born and when she had broken her arm playing second base on a softball team a few years before.

She typed the insurance company's address on a label and stuck it on a large brown envelope, then collected all of the forms and receipts into a neat pile. Normally her secretary would take over from here, but Cindy was the entire Personnel Department at the moment, so she would have to make the copies for her files. She stood up to go make the copies when the telephone rang.

"Personnel, Cindy Carroll speaking," she said into the mouthpiece, hoping the conversation would be brief so she could get the envelope into the mail before the five-o'clock pickup.

"Hi, Cindy. This is Preston Pearson."

"Oh, hi, Preston. What's up?"

"Nothing new," he said. "I just wanted to call and remind you about the charity ball tomorrow night. You're still going with me, aren't you?"

"Of course. I haven't forgotten."

"Great. We're counting on your notoriety to draw a crowd. Our publicity must be working because all the tickets have been sold."

"Are you going to set up my tent?"

"No. You won't have to do anything at the ball but have a good time. It should be an easy evening, no palm readings, no crystal ball, no tent. All we want you to do is circulate and spread goodwill—and look sexy, of course. I'll bet every red-blooded man there will want to dance with Madame Destiny."

"Watch what you say," she warned. "I wouldn't want anyone to overhear you calling me that."

"Don't worry," he said reassuringly, "I wouldn't do anything to upset our star attraction. I can recognize a gold mine when I see one."

"Only as long as the gold goes to the charity and no

one finds out who she really is. Once the mystery is gone, so is the magic—and so am I."

"I don't have to be psychic to know that. Your secret's safe with me."

"Good."

"Anyway, back to the reason I called. I've got a little surprise for you. Last month the committee voted to buy Madame Destiny a new dress so you won't have to keep borrowing that costume from the theater group. It'll be delivered either today or tomorrow."

"A new dress? Hey, thanks a lot. The old one is a little shabby. I think it was meant to be a witch's costume, and I always felt a little uncomfortable in it. But where on earth did you find an outfit that is suitable for, uh, you know who?"

"We did have a little trouble with that. There don't seem to be any fortune-tellers' boutiques in Petersburg. I suggested we look at one of the exotic lingerie stores—"

"Preston, you didn't!" Cindy exclaimed in horror.

"I tried," he said with an exaggerated sigh, "but I was outvoted. One of the committee women knows a dressmaker who donated her skills. All we had to do was furnish the material. I hope it will fit, because we won't have time for alterations before tomorrow night. Are you still a size five?"

"Yes, but how did you remember that? Even my grandmother has to ask my size every Christmas."

"Grandmothers don't notice gorgeous figures like guys do."

"Stop teasing me, Pres." Cindy felt herself blushing and was glad he couldn't see her.

65

"I can *hear* your cheeks getting pink," he said, joking mercilessly.

"You know me too well."

"But not well enough. Maybe tomorrow will be my lucky night."

"Don't forget that this is not really a date."

"Don't be such a spoilsport, Cindy," he retorted, but she could tell by his tone that he wasn't really disappointed. They had known each other for several years, but neither had ever tried to push their relationship beyond friendship. They were both too comfortable with things the way they were.

"The banquet starts at seven, so I'll pick you up about six-thirty, okay?" he asked, turning the subject back to business.

"That's fine. But come to the back entrance. There's no way I'll walk out the front door dressed like that."

"I understand. You're becoming something of a celebrity, in a weird way. Did you see that article about you in last Sunday's paper? You've got everyone guessing about your true identity."

"Let's keep it that way."

"Sure thing, Cindy. See you tomorrow."

She dropped the phone back into its cradle and hurried out of her office before it could ring again. Of course Madame Destiny would be there tomorrow night. The charity fund needed the money, and besides, Cindy didn't have any plans of her own.

No one else was using the machine, so she separated her forms into neat little piles and adjusted the first page facedown on the glass window. She had worked her way through three complete claims and part of a fourth when a little red light started flashing.

"Add toner," she said, reading the blinking signal aloud. It took her a couple of minutes to find a bottle of toner in the cabinet next to the machine. Opening the doors in front of the copier, she dumped the contents of the small bottle into the proper container, then pushed the reset button, closed the doors, and pressed the green space marked COPY.

The machine hummed and obediently spit another page into the collection tray. Cindy leaned over to see if it was dark enough, then groaned. The entire page was black. She pushed the button again, hoping the toner would filter more evenly, but the results were the same.

She exhaled in a tremendous sigh. Glancing at her watch, she saw that she had less than an hour to fix the machine, finish the job, and get the insurance papers into the mail. Again she opened the doors and knelt down to peer vaguely into the jumble of drums, rollers, and other unfamiliar mechanical parts.

Cindy could type ninety-eight words per minute, figure out most business-oriented computer programs in less than an hour, and make excellent coffee. But when it came to broken machinery, she was out of her line of expertise. Nothing looked any different than it had a few minutes before, when the machine had been operating properly. Experimentally she pushed a few things, pulled a few others, but nothing seemed to be out of place. She jiggled the toner container, hoping to redistribute it. Instead a small black cloud billowed out of the hole, settling in a fine mist on her hands and forearms.

"Yuck," she stated, staring at the mess.

"Need any help?"

Cindy let her head fall forward until her chin almost

touched her chest. Why did Nick have to come into this room at this moment? Why did he always have to catch her at her worst? She had wanted him to notice her for a long time, but did it always have to be when she was in some sort of distress? Hoping against hope that she had imagined his presence, she lifted her head and looked behind her.

He stood smiling down at her like a benevolent giant.

"This machine and I seem to be having a slight disagreement," she explained, holding her hands out for his examination. "I want my copies to be legible and it wants them to be black."

"Let me see if I can fix it." Shrugging out of his suit jacket, he placed it neatly over the back of a chair well away from the copy machine, then unbuttoned his cuffs and rolled up each sleeve to his elbows. Gingerly he bent down beside her, being careful not to let his knees touch the blackened floor.

Cindy watched as he pushed and pulled the same things she had, then tried to stop him as he began to jostle the toner container. It was all she could do to swallow the laughter that rose in her throat as a black cloud puffed up, then settled on Nick's tanned arms.

"You've already tried that, huh?" he asked, turning to her with an infectious grin on his lips.

"With the same results," she remarked, unable to hold back her laughter any longer.

"We make a fine team, don't we?" he said teasingly, shaking his hands. Though the black dust clung persistently, his smile never wavered. "Why don't you try it one more time? If all our mechanical genius hasn't fixed it, then I'll get my secretary to call the repairman."

She went through the motions again. She and Nick

68

watched expectantly as the light flashed beneath the cover and a perfectly printed page slid out.

"It works! Hey, we're better mechanics than we thought." Nick looked ruefully at his hands, then at hers. "Unfortunately neither of us can touch anything without leaving very unbusinesslike smudges."

"You're right. How am I ever going to finish this if I can't pick up the papers? I can't pick up the papers until I wash my hands and I can't leave these things here while I go wash my hands."

"Confidential files?"

"Insurance claims, but I wouldn't want anyone else to see them," she explained, her gaze searching the room for some paper towels or a rag so she could wipe the black powder off her hands.

"Would you trust me with them?" he asked, the joking edge never quite leaving his voice. "I'll stay here and guard them with my life until you get back. And I promise not to peek at anything."

Cindy met his twinkling cornflower-blue eyes and agreed with mock seriousness. "I'll be able to see your fingerprints on the pages if you do. If I can't trust the boss, then I can't trust anyone. But if you're sure you won't mind, I'll hurry."

"I'll be right here," he said, reassuring her.

When she glanced in the mirror over the sink as she scrubbed her hands, Cindy was dismayed to see that there were several smudges on her cheeks too. She could just imagine what he thought of her now. Wet dresses, messy hair, dirty face . . . Nick probably thought she was the sloppiest person in the world. She finished washing her hands and arms and wiped the marks off her face. Wishing she had some lip gloss with her, she did what she could without the help of a brush or comb to straighten her hair, then wet several towels for Nick and returned to the copy room.

"Do you need to use the copy machine?" she asked after handing him the towels.

Nick concentrated on wiping his hands clean as he tried to think of a good excuse. The truth was, he had been on his way to the accounting department when he had seen her go into the copy room. On an impulse he had followed her. But he couldn't come right out and tell her that. She might think he was interested in her.

Well, he was, wasn't he? Through a few discreet inquiries he had found out that she wasn't married, and as far as anyone knew, she wasn't seriously involved with anyone. Which meant that the way was open for him.

Then why was he suddenly dumbstruck with shyness? Those who knew Nick Wainwright well never would have believed he had a shy bone in his body. He was known for his witty repartee, but now he couldn't seem to put two intelligent words together. As casually as possible he leaned one hip against the copy machine and continued to rub his arms with the wet towels.

If he thought hard enough, he could probably come up with a convincing lie about why he had come into the copy room. But just as he had sensed that Cindy was different from most of the women he had been dating, he wanted his relationship with her to be different. After several hours of soul-searching the night before, it was clear to him that he did want to get to know her better, but if it was ever to mean anything more than just another fling, then it must be based on total honesty. Her openness and her lack of pretension were some of the reasons he was so attracted to her. She joked with him but didn't tease. She laughed with him but didn't flirt. He had no reason to believe that she had been anything but completely honest with him, and it wouldn't be fair for him to lie to her.

"Cindy, I . . ." he began, struggling to keep his voice steady. This honesty business was harder than he had thought. "I—actually I was going to stop by your office this afternoon to talk to you, but when I saw you come in here, I thought maybe we'd have a little more privacy and followed you." Whew! That had been tough. Raising his gaze until it met her questioning one, he watched for her reaction.

Cindy wasn't sure how she should interpret his words. Why had he wanted to talk to her? Why did he want privacy? Her heart hammered in her chest as she considered the range of options. It could be anything from a personnel question to a personal question. Of course, she hoped it was the latter, but the suspense was making her crazy.

"Did you want to ask me about someone who works here?" Nervously she fumbled with the paper clip as she finished another file and reached for a new set of completed forms to copy.

"Yes, I do. A Miss Cynthia Carroll," he answered with a tentative smile, wondering if this odd sensation he was feeling could be blamed on the vibration of the machine he was leaning against or on the pretty lady standing in front of him.

"Me?" She practically melted beneath the intensity of his blue eyes.

"Yes, you. I'd like to know if you're busy Saturday

night. I thought maybe we could go out to eat or see a movie."

"Saturday night?" she repeated weakly. Preston's voice penetrated her consciousness, reminding her that she would be at the benefit ball until very late tomorrow night, which would leave no time for an extra date . . . especially one she had been waiting for for ten years. But she had already made a commitment to Preston, and as much as she hated to do it, she would have to turn Nick down.

"I can't this Saturday. I've already made other plans," she answered, trying to make her voice reflect how very sorry she was that she couldn't accept his offer.

"Oh . . . well, I guess I should have expected that. It was such short notice." Nick shrugged with a nonchalance he wasn't feeling. It had been stupid of him to think that a desirable woman like her wouldn't already have a date. He shouldn't be so impatient, he reminded himself. After all, they had only met the day before. But after the bizarre buildup by that even more bizarre fortune-teller, he couldn't help but be eager to get to know the woman who might be his perfect mate.

Why didn't he ask her out tonight? Cindy's fingers automatically crossed in a superstitious plea for good luck. She wasn't busy tonight, her heart cried. Should she be an eighties woman and suggest it herself? No, not with him. She felt like she had manipulated the situation enough already. From here on she had to let him make all the first moves. If anything did develop between them, she would tell him the truth about Madame Destiny, and she didn't want him to have any reason to think he had been railroaded.

Nick continued in his effort to clean his hands but seemed to be smearing more than he was removing. He wanted to ask her out tonight, but if she was like any of the other women he knew, she would be insulted at the idea that he would wait to the last minute. He stepped away from the machine and tossed the dirty towels in the trash can. Oh, well, he could spend the weekend looking at houses with his realtor. He had been trying to find the time, and it looked like he would have it now.

"Maybe some other time." He hid his disappointment behind a dazzling smile.

"Yes, some other time," Cindy echoed dully as he picked up his jacket between his two cleanest fingertips and walked out the door.

"Darn it!" she exclaimed as she replaced the page she had just printed and shut the cover with a thud. Was she doomed to spend the rest of her life watching him leave?

She missed the mail run. In fact, all the complications in the copy room had delayed her so much that it was after six o'clock when she finally turned out her office lights and locked her door. The parking lot was empty except for her yellow compact car. Cindy tossed her purse and the brown insurance envelope onto the passenger seat as she slid behind the steering wheel.

It had been an exhausting week, and she was anxious to get to her apartment, relax in a long, hot bath, and take a good book to bed. Kay was working on rehearsals and wouldn't be home until very late, so Cindy would have plenty of time alone to wonder how this week, which could have been so right, had turned out so wrong.

Stabbing the key into the ignition, she turned it, expecting to hear the car's engine roar to life. Instead only a funny clicking sound met her ears. She tried again, then once more until even the clicking weakened. It couldn't be out of gas because she had just filled it up that morning. The battery had to be dead.

But could one die so quickly without any warning symptoms? The battery was as old as her car, and for all she knew about batteries, six years might be a ripe old age . . . forty-two in dog years. It might have been the Methuselah of batteries. She realized she was verging on hysteria, which wouldn't help her predicament at all. Leaning forward until her head rested against the steering wheel, Cindy wondered what could possibly go wrong next.

She would have to walk at least a mile in her high heels to the nearest telephone so she could call a taxi, that's what. If only she hadn't been the last person to leave the building, she could have gone back inside and used her office phone. But the heavy glass entrance doors had locked behind her when she left. She had even checked it to make sure, even though she knew that after five P.M. it was always set on automatic so that people could leave but no one could enter. And since the company was so far from town and it was so late, the few other offices that were in this area already would have closed too. And the thought of hitchhiking, even in this friendly city, scared her to death.

She didn't know how long she sat there trying to psych herself up. It didn't help that the sky was overcast, definitely threatening rain soon. But when she noticed that because of the clouds it was beginning to get dark earlier than usual, she decided it was time to take a hike. She had just gathered up her purse, the envelope, and an umbrella when a sleek black car zipped into the parking lot, screeching to a stop in front of the building.

Cindy watched Nick's tall, athletic form unfold from the depths of the low-slung car with mixed emotions. She wasn't sure whether she was feeling relief or dismay at his unexpected appearance. Of course, she was always thrilled to see him and she did need help, but did the circumstances always have to make her look so inadequate?

"What are you doing here so late?" he asked as soon as he was close enough for her to hear. "Either I'm not paying you enough for you to afford a place to live or I'm working you too many hours. Which is it?"

"Neither." She surprised herself with a genuine laugh. "My car wasn't as anxious to leave the parking lot as I was. I think the battery's dead."

"Boy, you're heck on machinery. Remind me never to let you near my antique jukebox."

"I admit that this hasn't been one of my better days."

"Would you like me to see if I can find out what's wrong with it?" he asked, eyeing her aging car dubiously.

"Do you know any more about fixing cars than you do about copy machines?"

"No, not much," he admitted. "I know how to pump gas and change a tire, but I'm not very mechanically inclined."

"Forget it, then. I'll get my dad to come over and look at it tomorrow." They started walking across the parking lot toward the building. "Why are you here?" she asked.

"To pick up some papers I forgot. I'm working on a

75

special design for a new line of pens, and since it looks like I'll have a lot of free time this weekend, I thought I could do some work on it."

Cindy suspected he was referring to her earlier rejection, but she couldn't tell if he was serious or just joking about it. "I can't believe you'll be sitting at home alone long enough to get any real work done," she bantered, keeping her tone light.

"After you turned me down I lost all my self-confidence and couldn't get up enough nerve to call anyone else." He thrust his hands deep into his pockets and looked down at the tips of his black shoes, pretending to be overcome with shyness.

"Oh, sure." She gave him a doubtful look. "Somehow you don't strike me as the type of man who takes no for an answer."

"Sometimes I don't have a choice." Lifting his head, his warm blue eyes met hers in a silent appeal.

"Well, if you'll be kind enough to unlock the front door so I can call a taxi, I'll leave you alone. The evening is still young, and you might suddenly remember the phone number of some gorgeous young thing who doesn't know how to say no." Suddenly very flustered, Cindy realized that when it came to flirting with Nick, she was an amateur. It was so much easier when so much of her happiness didn't rest in the balance.

Nick took a ring of keys out of his pocket and flipped through them until he found the one that fit the front door. But instead of opening it he turned to face her, blocking her path.

"You don't have to call a cab. Just give me a couple of minutes to get my papers and I'll run you home in my car," he offered.

76

"Oh, no, you don't have to go out of your way. I don't mind taking a taxi."

"It won't take me long. You'll be home before the cab could even get here. They're so slow that you'll probably be late for whatever you're planning to do tonight."

"There's nothing happening this evening that I could be late for," she answered honestly.

"No date? No important plans?"

"No, nothing," she repeated.

"Good. Then there's no reason why you should pay all that money and waste all that time with a cab when I'm here, is there?" he said, a note of challenge in his voice.

It was a reasonable solution to her problem. Why shouldn't she accept his offer? She could think of several dozen reasons why she would love to. The thought of riding through town with him in that sexy car left her slightly breathless. If only she lived farther from the office so she could spend even more time with him.

"If you're sure it's no trouble, then I'd appreciate a ride to my apartment," she answered finally. The shyness in her voice was genuine.

"Great," he responded, reassuring her with a wide, warm smile. Again he reached into his pocket and pulled out a key case and separated a round key from the rest. "Here's the key to the car doors." Casting a quick, appraising glance up at the darkened sky, he went on. "You'd probably better wait for me inside the car in case the weather breaks before I get back."

"I promise not to touch anything mechanical. Considering my track record today, your car probably wouldn't start, either." She exchanged a mischievous grin for the keys.

77

"You can spill water on my pants, you can break my copy machine, but *please* don't hurt my new car," he pleaded with mock horror. "I've only had it for a couple of months. I haven't even had to refill the windshield washer yet."

"I'll keep my hands to myself," she vowed solemnly, her hazel eyes wide with affected innocence.

"Darn!" he exclaimed, and added with a slow, teasing wink, "Now you really have ruined my evening."

CHAPTER FIVE

The plush tan leather seats were as luxurious as Cindy had imagined. But that pleasure was nothing compared to how great it felt being isolated with Nick in the compact interior of his car. He was so close that if she hadn't been sitting so tightly in the middle of her seat, their arms could have touched easily.

Obviously he had had enough time to go to his house and take a shower. His shiny brown hair had recently been washed and had barely had time to dry. He had changed out of his business clothes and was wearing jeans and a bright red polo shirt that looked fantastic with his tanned skin and dark hair. A faint, clean smell of soap combined with his after-shave drifted over to her sensitive nostrils. Not even the delicious fragrance of her mother's freshly baked chocolate-chip cookies could compare with the intoxicating smell of this man.

As he maneuvered the car around a sharp curve Cindy tightened her grip on her purse and felt the stiff paper of the brown envelope.

"Oh, I almost forgot. If it's not too much trouble, could we drop this by the post office? It's those insurance forms I was working on this afternoon, and I really would like to get them in the mail tonight. It's only a few blocks out of the way." Since it was company business, she hoped he wouldn't mind. She didn't want to take it home with her for fear it might get misplaced. Besides, it was a good excuse to spend a few extra minutes with Nick.

"No problem," he responded with an agreeable grin. He downshifted as he made another turn, but his mind was not on the smooth way his car was handling. He was trying to decide whether or not he should take a chance and ask her to join him for dinner tonight. Considering the reputation that had preceded him and the fact that they barely knew each other—something he wanted to change as soon as possible—he was afraid she might think he was coming on too strong too soon, and run in the opposite direction. She had already turned him down once, and even though he had no reason to suspect that she didn't actually have plans, his suddenly fragile ego couldn't take another no from her just yet.

Daring a glance at her, he was again struck by how different he felt with her compared to other women he had dated. Though he seemed to catch her in awkward situations, he had no doubt that she was a strong, self-sufficient woman, capable of taking care of herself. But there was also a guilelessness about her, an innocence of spirit that had nothing to do with naïveté.

It could be her adorable face with its lively, youthful quality that would probably keep her looking years younger than her actual age all her life. Though he knew she was in her mid-twenties, he wouldn't be surprised if she still occasionally got carded at clubs and bars. Or it could be her petiteness that made him feel bigger and more protective than usual. Or perhaps it was her cheerful, easygoing attitude that he found so delightful. It could be any or all those things that attracted him to her, but whatever the reason, he was definitely attracted.

He turned his attention back to the road seconds before Cindy sneaked a sideways look at him. It didn't appear that he had any formal plans for the evening. Should she ask him into her apartment when they got there? Should she ask him to stay for dinner? Kay wouldn't be there. Then she remembered that unless Kay had gone shopping in the last twenty-four hours, the only thing in their freezer was a pizza, a package of raspberry fruit bars, and half a package of fish sticks—certainly nothing worth serving to the most gorgeous man in Virginia.

"Are you planning on going to the company's Fourth of July picnic?" he asked.

"Oh, sure," she answered, savoring the deep warmth of his voice. "They're always a lot of fun, especially if we can get enough people to drag themselves away from the food long enough to play a game of softball."

"You like sports?"

"Some, especially when it's one I can play. But I have yet to be contacted by any baseball scouts."

Their laughter filled the small car, making it seem even more intimate than before.

"What position do you play? Shortstop?" His eyes twinkled as he asked.

"Shame on you! A 'short' joke," she sputtered, pretending to be insulted.

"I'm sorry. It was a cheap shot, I admit, but you started it."

He steered the car into the post office drive and stopped close enough to the box so that Cindy could drop the envelope in without getting out of the car. That chore finished, he headed the car back toward the road but stopped again before entering the busy flow of Friday evening traffic. Turning to look at Cindy, he decided he had better ask her now.

"Since neither of us have anything special to do tonight, why don't we go get something to eat? It'll be my treat to make up for my rude joke." That was good, he congratulated himself. Nice and light. She couldn't possibly be frightened away by such a casual invitation.

Actually she was ecstatic. It took all her self-control to keep her voice calm as she accepted with a cool, "Sure. That would be nice."

"I'm not dressed for anything fancy," he commented, glancing down at his jeans.

"Good, because after the day I had today, I'm not in the mood for anything too demanding."

They finally settled on pizza, and Nick drove to the Italian restaurant she recommended.

"I've been away from here too long to know what's going on in this town anymore. Most of my old haunts have either gone out of business or been turned into video stores." Nick sprinkled parmesan cheese on his salad as he continued nostalgically. "There used to be a drive-in hamburger stand right where this building is now. My buddies and I spent many an hour here drinking soda and watching the girls." He sighed. "I was born and raised in Petersburg, but I feel like a stranger in my own hometown."

"I was born here, too, but since I've never lived anywhere else and the changes have been so gradual, I haven't paid much attention."

They continued to compare notes on how their city

had evolved over the years. They didn't notice when the tapered red candle stuck in a wine bottle flickered and burned itself out or when the rain finally came, pelting against the windows. The pizza disappeared much too quickly, and as dozens of other couples who had arrived after them began leaving, Cindy and Nick knew they had lingered long enough.

Once the ice had broken between them, neither of them could stop talking. It seemed a natural progression for Cindy to invite Nick into her apartment as he parked next to her building, an automatic and apt response for him to accept.

"Where are you living now, Nick? Did you find an apartment near the office?" Cindy's question was muffled as she moved around in the kitchen, rinsing out the coffeepot before she measured fresh grounds into the machine. After plugging it in she got two mismatched coffee mugs out of the cabinet.

"I'm still living at home with my mother and sister," he replied. "My old room was always ready and waiting for me every time I came back to town, so it seemed the most logical place for me to stay. After Dad's funeral Mom seemed to need me for a while. But lately she's been getting out more and learning to adjust, so I'm going to start looking for a place of my own soon. I've been talking to a realtor, and she's watching out for a nice house on a little land that I can afford."

"So you're really going all the way to settle down here, then? Buying a house is a major step toward losing your freedom, you know."

"Yes, I know."

Cindy jumped, and the mugs rattled together noisily. His voice was much closer than she had expected. She had thought he was still waiting for her in the living room.

"I've been thinking a lot about settling down lately. I think it's time," he continued, walking farther into the small kitchen until almost her entire vision was filled with him.

It was odd that when she and Kay were working in there together it never felt so crowded. Nick's height, his broad, muscular shoulders, and overwhelming masculine presence made the room seem incredibly tiny.

"Oh?" she whispered weakly.

"I think it suddenly dawned on me that I was twenty-eight years old, had had the advantage of an excellent education and didn't have a damn thing to show for it. All of my friends here are married, some for the second time, and most of them have a kid or two."

"The old biological clock syndrome?" she asked with a gentle, understanding smile.

"Something like that, I guess. I think it had a lot to do with my dad dying so suddenly. He wasn't even fifty years old. When I looked at the company he had built from absolutely nothing, with all its employees and their families he had been responsible for, not to mention his own family, I felt totally useless. I couldn't think of a single thing I had ever done for anyone else. I've lived my life for myself. I haven't done anything I'm ashamed of, but it's time I grew up and took on some responsibilities.

"Now that I own the company with my mother, brother, and sister," he went on, resting a hand on the cabinet door next to her and tilting his head so that he was looking down at her in an unconsciously appealing

84

pose, "a part of me is satisfied. But there's still something missing from my life. . . ."

"Oh?" she repeated, even fainter than before. She seemed to be having a great deal of difficulty breathing regularly, and she had no idea what wild rhythm her heart was pounding out against her chest.

"I've been hoping I'd meet a woman that would make me want to settle down and maybe start a family of my own."

"And have you?" she squeaked. "Met this woman, I mean?"

"I'm not sure yet. But I think so." He leaned closer.

Cindy swallowed hard. This was the moment she had been waiting for, but now that it was about to happen, she was scared to death. What if his kiss did nothing for her?

His head was slowly bending toward her.

What if he was rough and his lips were hard? What if she absolutely hated every second of it? Trivial when compared to world peace or nuclear waste, but the next few minutes could shatter every adolescent dream and fantasy she had ever had about Nicholas Wainwright. It was even more frightening to think that she might fall instantly in love but that Nick would be disappointed in her and leave her life as quickly as he had entered it.

Nick's breath was warm against her face. A thick lock of dark brown hair fell across his forehead and brushed against her bangs.

What if—

All her arguments were forgotten as his lips met hers. They lightly brushed across her mouth, teasing and tasting until she relaxed and lifted her face up to his. His arms slid around her waist, pulling her gently against the solid length of his body. She could feel his heartbeat speed up as his mouth closed more firmly over hers, deepening their kiss.

All logical thoughts fled her mind as the tip of his tongue followed the tender curve of her lips before sliding inside to explore the warm depths of her mouth. Desire, more powerful and wonderful than she had ever imagined, spiraled through her limbs, settling deep in the pit of her stomach. Her hands delighted in the extravagance of being able to caress his shoulders and follow the curve of his neck into the silken depths of his hair.

All sense of time vanished as they clung to each other, taking and giving with a passion neither of them had suspected they would share.

"Oh, Cindy." He breathed heavily against the soft crown of her head as he held her possessively in the circle of his arms. "Do you have any idea what you've done to me? Are you feeling this too?"

She couldn't speak, as her head rested against his shoulder. Her legs were so weak, she could barely stand, even with his support, but she managed to nod in answer to his question. Yes, she was feeling it, from the top of her head where his chin was resting, to the tips of her toes, which were still curled from the potency of his kisses.

Oh, Lord, how he wanted her. She aroused emotions in him that he had never felt before. His body ached with a physical desire to possess her while his heart felt like it would burst from the joy of holding her in his arms. He sensed she would let him go as far as he wanted, sharing this newly discovered passion until they were both satisfied, at least temporarily. But his need for her was more than just physical. What he felt for her was so different and wondrous that he didn't want to do anything to undermine it.

He hadn't had this intensity or excitement since the first time he had thought he had fallen in love with a girl during high school. There was something so extraordinary about that sensation that he had never expected to feel it again. But here he was, holding the sweetest, most fascinating woman he had ever met and talking himself out of taking her to bed because he cared too much. That was definitely a new experience for him.

Tenderly he held her until their breathing returned to normal and their hearts settled down. Nick was carrying on a silent debate with himself about whether or not he should tell her about this wonderful rebirth he was experiencing with her. But he was still a little skeptical, and his well-honed bachelor wariness won out. He decided to wait until he was absolutely certain about how far he wanted this relationship to go.

"Is that coffee ready yet?" he asked, gruffly clearing his throat as he took a small step backward.

Cindy shared his feelings of confusion and was almost grateful for the physical distance between them. She still felt like she was involved in an incredible dream, fearful that she would awaken. She wasn't ready for this moment, whether it was a dream or reality, to end yet. But she didn't want to give him the wrong impression about her, either. If she appeared too eager, he might think she reacted this way to every guy she dated. He had no way of knowing how special he was to her, and she couldn't tell him just yet or he would think she was trying to trap him. If only he knew the whole truth. But she couldn't tell him that, either.

"It should be." She picked up the mugs and walked to the coffeepot. The thin stream of freshly brewed liquid trickled to a stop as she reached for the pot.

"Cindy, do you believe in destiny?"

The pot slipped from her suddenly nerveless fingers. Luckily it settled back into its molded warming pad without breaking or spilling.

"Destiny?" She swallowed back her heart, which seemed to have leapt into her throat. "What do you mean?"

"Oh, you know, fate, kismet, predestination. The weird feeling you get when something happens that you knew ahead of time was going to happen. Something that feels so right that you just know it was meant to be."

"Would you rather have green or yellow?" she asked, trying desperately to avoid the most uncomfortable subject he possibly could have brought up.

"What?"

"Green or yellow?" she repeated, holding out the filled mugs.

He shrugged. "It doesn't matter. Green, I guess." He accepted the mug she held out for him and followed her back into the living room.

Settling on the brown tweed couch, he watched her as she left her mug on the coffee table and crossed the room to the stereo. Slipping a cassette into the slot, she punched a button and the sounds of soft rock filled the room.

"Have you ever had your palm read?" Nick inquired,

continuing the line of questioning that was so dominant in his mind.

The question startled Cindy so much that her hand slipped across the volume knob, sending a surge of music vibrating through the room. Quickly she turned it back down to a low, background level as her thoughts scrambled to come up with a reason for his persistence.

All evening she had been feeling a little guilty about the deception that had helped bring them together. Did he suspect something? Was he merely curious about her opinions on these subjects? Or could that be too much of a coincidence? They had had such a good time this evening, and he had a really terrific sense of humor. If she confessed to him now that she, as Madame Destiny, had sort of guided Cupid's arrow, he might think it was a good joke and get a big laugh out of it.

Or he could, since he still didn't know her extremely well, think that she had tampered with fate and angrily leave before she had a chance to fully explain her reasons. Until she felt more confident about their relationship, she couldn't share her secret with him.

"Although I believe it's possible for people to have psychic powers, I'm not sure I want to get involved with them," she replied at last, skillfully avoiding his question as she joined him on the couch.

"You couldn't find a person more doubtful than me when it comes to things like astrology and numerology, but I had the strangest experience with a fortune-teller last weekend. Did you go to the charity carnival last Saturday?"

Now how should she answer that? Of course she was there, but she hadn't actually circulated among the booths or strayed far from the tent except to go to the bathroom and get a hot dog. "I wanted to go, but something came up," she said with a weak smile.

"I'm almost ashamed to admit it, but I had my palm read by a lady called Madame Destiny, and she was incredibly accurate. I'll tell you more about it sometime," he promised, hesitant to tell her that his fortune had included her. Instead Nick's gaze swept over Cindy's shiny, reddish-gold hair, then across the delicate features of her face, pausing with extra interest on the soft, red fullness of her lips and her large, expressive eyes. "You have the most beautiful eyes I've ever seen," he murmured. "They're such an incredible shade of green with little gold streaks in them."

"Thanks," she said, breathing a silent sigh of relief that he had strayed off the subject of Madame Destiny. "But I have to give partial credit to my contact lenses. Actually my eyes are a rather ordinary hazel, neither green nor brown. It's sort of like my genes couldn't quite decide which one would dominate, so they take turns. So when I turned in my glasses for contacts, the doctor talked me into wearing green ones that give my eyes more color."

Whatever else he would have said was interrupted by a loud knock on the front door.

Cindy automatically glanced at her watch and saw that it was after nine o'clock. It was too early for Kay and too late for unexpected visitors. "Who could that be?" she asked rhetorically as she stood up and went to answer the summons.

"This delivery came for you today and I forgot all about it until a few minutes ago when Fred went to get his bathrobe and saw it lying on the dresser." Cindy's landlady, Gladys, stood in the hallway holding a large white box as she skipped a formal greeting and ran on with her explanation. "I would have waited until the morning, but then I figured it might be something important, since you two girls don't get many deliveries here, so I just brought it right up. I'm glad you're not in bed yet." Gladys's gaze slid over Cindy's shoulder and settled on Nick. Her gasp was audible all the way across the room. "Oh, dear, I hope I haven't interrupted anything," she said, but clearly she would have been more pleased if she had.

"No. This is my boss, Nicholas Wainwright," Cindy explained, trying not to laugh at the old woman's horrified but curious expression. Gladys had never made the transition into the more liberal eighties and assumed that her renters hadn't, either, which in Cindy's and Kay's cases wasn't far from the truth. Since moving in over a year before, neither of them had entertained a man in the apartment for anything more intimate than a dinner or a heated game of backgammon.

"I worked late this evening, and when my car wouldn't start, he kindly brought me home," she said, continuing her explanation and opening the door wider so Gladys could get a full view without getting a neck cramp. Nick smiled and nodded a friendly greeting as he sipped the hot coffee.

It all looked so perfectly innocent that even Gladys's suspicious mind was satisfied. She handed Cindy the box and left the two young people alone again.

The name printed in black ink on the corner of the box was unfamiliar to her, but since she was expecting no other packages, she assumed it must be the dress Preston had told her about. She was practically dying of curiosity, but she knew she couldn't open it in front of Nick.

"A present from a secret admirer?" he asked, hoping his voice didn't contain any hints of the jealousy that was stirring within him. He, too, had seen the name on the corner of the box and recognized it as an expensive seamstress his mother and sister often used for special occasions. Who dared send *his* Cindy a present as personal as a piece of clothing?

"Not really. It's just a dress," she answered quickly.

"Aren't you going to open it?"

"No, not right now."

"But—"

"I'm going to take it to my bedroom. I'll be right back." Before he could say anything else, she hurried from the room with the box in her arms. She managed to take a peek before she put it on a shelf in her closet. The sight of a lot of black lace and sequins made her long to take it out and try it on, but she didn't dare as long as Nick was sitting in the next room. She would have time later for a more thorough inspection.

When she returned to the living room, she saw that Nick had walked over to her bookcases and was reading the titles she had lined up on the shelves.

"Hey," he exclaimed when he heard her rejoin him. "You've got some old copies of the Missile. Do you mind if I look at them?"

"No, go ahead."

"Lord, it's been years since I've seen this," he said as he ran his hands over the smooth crimson-and-gold cover of the Petersburg High School yearbook. "Nineteen seventy-seven. That was the year I graduated."

He didn't have to tell Cindy that.

92

"Look, it opened right to the page that has my graduation picture on it. Have you ever seen such an awful photograph? I can't believe I ever wore my hair that long."

Cindy thought it was a terrific picture and remembered how attractive she had thought he looked with his hair hanging across his forehead like that. Of course, he was even more handsome now, but she had never had any complaints about the way he looked.

"Man, does this bring back the memories. Look, there's the football team. There's Mike and Rick and Bobby . . . and there's me, trying to look lean and mean."

"You were the greatest quarterback Petersburg High ever had. Number twelve, the Crimson Mystic," she said before realizing how revealing her memories were.

"That was my number—and my nickname. How did you know that?"

"I—I don't know how I remembered that after all these years," she said, stammering, trying to cover her slipup. "Where did you get that nickname?"

He shrugged modestly and gazed at the glossy black-and-white pictures on the page. "I can't remember exactly when my teammates came up with it, but they used to joke that I hypnotized our opponents so they never even saw the ball zip over their heads when I passed it. Having magical powers would have been nice, but it had more to do with having a pretty good passing arm than any spells. I was at the peak of my ability then, and I had a lot of good receivers."

"But you went on to play ball at college, too, didn't you?" She knew most of the story secondhand, but she wanted to hear it from his point of view.

"Yes. I went to the University of Alabama on an athletic scholarship, but it was a whole different ball game there. The competition was tougher, not only with our opponents but also with the other U of A athletes trying to make the team. It didn't take me long to find out I didn't have the killer instinct it would take to make it in the big time. I loved playing in high school, but there was too much pressure playing for such a major college. Thousands of people, not to mention those who watched national television, took winning so seriously that it drained some of the fun of the sport for me. I had to give one hundred and ten percent all of the time just to stay on the team and keep up my grades. But it meant so much to my dad that I stuck with it."

He paused, unconsciously flexing his right arm. "Then, in my senior year, I got sandwiched between some heavyweight Baylor linebackers at the Cotton Bowl. My arm pads got torn off, and when they threw me down, I landed smack on my elbow. If you've ever hit your elbow, you've probably wondered why they call it a funny bone, because it hurts like heck. Breaking it hurts even worse. I didn't think it would ever get well. My arm was in a cast for a couple of months, and after that it seemed I had lost a lot of my strength and flexibility. I couldn't throw the bullet like I used to, and the pro teams lost interest in me. They had too much other talent to choose from.

"But it was odd," he continued with an almost bemused smile. "When I found out I wouldn't be going pro, it was almost a relief. I hadn't realized how pressured I had been feeling until I got hurt and my chances were ruined. I didn't have to worry about getting cut from the team, or going to endless practices, sweating

94

off five pounds a day out in the hot sun. For the first time in years I felt free to make my own choices. But I didn't realize until I graduated that I had no idea what to do next. I stumbled around for a few years until fate seemed to step in and decide my future for me. And that's how the Crimson Mystic became a ballpoint-pen magnate."

Turning his attention from his memories long enough to study her face, he shook his head as if to bring himself back to the present. "But that's enough about me. Tell me why you have this annual. Did you graduate from PHS?"

"Class of 1980."

"So you were a freshman when I was a senior. Let's see your picture." He started flipping pages, searching for the freshmen.

"Oh, no, you don't," she said with a gasp, trying to grab the book away from him, but he just lifted it out of her reach. Stretching and twisting, she kept trying to get it from him as he playfully backed away from her until the back of his legs touched the couch and he sat down, reaching out and pulling her down next to him.

"It couldn't be that bad considering how good you look now." The annual was cradled on his lap, and he continued to turn the pages with his right hand while his left arm wrapped around her shoulders, holding her against him.

"It's worse than bad. It's criminal. It looks like a mug shot." She continued to protest halfheartedly, but her mind couldn't really focus on anything else but how perfectly her body fit against his.

"Here it is," he crowed triumphantly, his finger pointing to a small black-and-white photo of a very young-looking girl with long hair and a wide smile. "It's not a bad picture. You look very . . . cute."

"Oh, please, not *cute.*"

"How about adorable, then?"

"I looked like I was about twelve years old. And look at those horn-rimmed glasses. I thought they made me look so intelligent."

"You looked gorgeous in a young, intelligent sort of way," he insisted. "I still can't believe that we went to the same school and I never noticed you."

They'd worked at the same company together for six months and he hadn't noticed her then, either, she thought. "There were probably close to two thousand students going to PHS back then. I wasn't a cheerleader or a class president or anything important like that. In fact, I was practically invisible. I can't imagine why you would have noticed me."

"Well, I've noticed you now," he whispered, lifting his hand to cup her face and turn it toward him.

His lips captured hers in a sweetly seductive kiss that made her feel like the most cherished woman in the world. It didn't matter if he thought she was cute or adorable or even gorgeous . . . as long as he kept kissing her like this.

"Just think of all the years we've wasted," Nick murmured huskily against her soft lips. "And all the time we could have had together."

Cindy already had.

CHAPTER SIX

The dress for Madame Destiny was beautiful. It had a long, form-fitting black satin slip with a low-cut *V* neckline, held up by sequined spaghetti straps. A floor-length, shimmering raschel lace gown of the same intensely dark shade fit over the slip. Its high neckline of scalloped lace fluffing beneath Cindy's chin would have looked demure if it hadn't been for the transparency of the lace, which displayed much more of her chest than it appeared at first glance.

Long, lacy sleeves hugged Cindy's slim arms, ending in deep points that dipped across the tops of her hands, almost to her fingers. The loosely flowing skirt swirled around her legs, the points of its handkerchief hem not quite touching the floor.

All in all, it was much too sexy and risqué for Cindy Carroll but just perfect for Madame Destiny. Kay fastened the sequined belt in the back, and Cindy stepped into her black high heels, her toes barely peeking out from under the hem. She walked over to the mirror to admire her new outfit.

"It's really fantastic, isn't it?" she asked breathlessly. The slim lines of the dress made her look tall and elegant, and perversely she wished Nick could see her in it.

But, of course, that was out of the question, for a while longer, anyway. It was a shame, however, that he wouldn't know what he was missing.

"It's the most gorgeous dress I've ever seen, and you look wonderful in it," Kay complimented. "Anytime you decide you're tired of being Madame Destiny, just let me know and I'll be glad to take over for you. Although how I'm going to get my size-ten body into that size-five dress is a mystery even Madame Destiny couldn't answer."

"I've revised my whole attitude toward Madame Destiny." Cindy laughed as she whirled in front of the mirror, watching how the lights were captured and held in the material's ebony folds. "She's changed my life. I take back every bad thought I've ever had and every bad word I've ever said about having to dress up and read strange, sweaty palms. I've never been happier, and I owe it all to Madame Destiny's brilliant plan."

"I can see that I'm going to have to put more makeup on you to tone down the glow of your face. It's positively blinding," Kay said teasingly. "Did something happen last night that you haven't told me about?"

When Kay had come home late the night before, she had found Cindy and Nick still sitting on the couch, surrounded by all four of the Missile annuals Cindy had. But it had been obvious by the well-kissed look on both their faces that they had not spent all their time reminiscing.

They had been very surprised to see her. Between nuzzles they had talked about everything from how bad the cafeteria food at PHS used to be to the new pen design Nick was working on. Neither had so much as glanced at their watches for the last three or four hours,

98

and they had been shocked at how much time had passed since Nick had brought her home.

"Oh, Kay, it was absolutely the best evening. I can't remember spending so much time on a date talking."

"Talking? It looked like the two of you had been doing a lot more than talking."

"Well, I will admit that our lips were pretty busy. But Nick was a perfect gentleman."

"Why do I get the impression that you were a little disappointed with that?" Kay's eyes sparkled devilishly.

"I had expected more from a man with his reputation. Somehow I thought I would have to be firm but kind as I patiently explained that I wasn't that type of woman. But he was so sweet and gentle, and so sexy, that if the subject does come up, I might forget to say no."

"Just be careful. I'd hate to see you get hurt if things don't turn out the way you hope."

"I'm trying to remind myself that there are no guarantees. Everything's going so great that it almost scares me. I keep waiting for the alarm to go off and wake me from this fantastic dream. But as long as it lasts, I'm going to make the most of it."

"And what about Nick?"

"He told me he feels the same way and wishes we could spend more time together. I know tonight's for a special cause, but I would rather be with him."

"You're going to be too busy dancing holes in your shoes even to think about Nicholas Wainwright tonight," Kay stated with conviction as she stared at her friend.

"I doubt that. But at least I have tomorrow to look

forward to. We're going for a drive in the country and a picnic."

"And here I was hoping you and I could ride our bikes to the park," Kay teased.

"Oh, Kay, I'm sorry. Why don't you go with us? I'm sure Nick wouldn't mind, and I—"

"No thanks." Kay shook her head emphatically. "There's no way you could talk me into being a tag-along on one of your dates. I saw the way the two of you were looking at each other last night, and what you don't need is a spectator. Besides, I don't think either of you would even remember I was along."

"Maybe next time we can plan a double date. I'm sure Nick has an unattached friend."

"Now that's an offer I couldn't refuse. But, honestly, I'm thrilled that you and Nick finally got together. If you weren't my best friend, I'd be envious. How many people get a second chance to experience the excitement of a first love?"

"That's what it feels like. My skin tingles and my heart feels like it's going to swell up and explode every time I'm near him. And when he kisses me . . ."

Kay's answer was a wistful sigh.

Cindy looked at the clock and realized she would have to hurry. Preston was the most punctual person she knew, and she didn't want him to have to wait for her. "They even made a matching veil to help hide my face. Would you help me pin it on before I leave?" she asked, searching for a few hairpins.

It was almost six-thirty when she opened the door to her apartment. Her hand rested on the doorjamb as she peeked warily up and down the hallway to make certain no one would see her. It was all clear, and she started to step out when a greenish-red sparkle caught her eye.

"Oh, no. I almost forgot to take off my ring," she exclaimed, quickly pulling the alexandrite off her finger.

"Let me have it," Kay offered. "I'll put it in your jewelry box for you."

"Thanks. I hate to think what would happen if someone I knew recognized that ring. As soon as anyone realizes Madame Destiny is really just an ordinary unpsychic, assistant personnel director, her credibility will be shot."

"But imagine how it would spice up your reputation if anyone recognized you while you were wearing that dress. You'd attract every eligible male for miles around."

"There's only one eligible male I want to attract, and I want to attract him as myself, not as Madame Destiny."

"Knock 'em dead."

"Thanks—I think."

Cindy's vision was only slightly impaired by the gauzy black lace that covered her head, falling in soft folds to just below her chin. From her place at the head table on a dais that ran the width of the room, she had an excellent view of the entire ballroom and its occupants.

A local hotel had donated the facilities and set up long tables stretching in red, linen-covered fingers from the main table. An area at the opposite end of the room had been left open for the dance that would follow the banquet. The walls were decorated with pictures that had been blown up into poster-sized prints of the vari-

101

ous disasters for which the charity had provided emergency aid.

Though Cindy was not a speaker, she had been seated in a place of honor between Preston and the mayor of Petersburg. She would have preferred not sitting next to Felicia's father, but he seemed pleasant enough and she tried to put aside her personal feelings for the evening.

Almost everyone had found a place to sit, and the noise of scraping chairs replaced the earlier buzz of conversation. Preston was pointing out a particularly generous benefactor when Cindy's attention was distracted by some late arrivals. A tall, dark-haired man with a chic blond beauty practically glued to his side hesitated in the doorway, searching for their table assignment.

From a distance Cindy knew it was Nick and Felicia even before the mayor rose and motioned for them to come closer. Cindy hadn't really paid attention to the two empty seats at the table almost directly in front of her. Apparently they had been reserved by the mayor for his daughter and her date.

Her date! Cindy fumed. How dare Nick ask Felicia out after last night? Hadn't it meant anything to him? Hadn't he felt the special bond that had been created by those hours of sharing memories and personal thoughts and dreams—not to mention those wonderful kisses? What kind of a fickle man was he?

She had to pull herself together, she thought, scolding herself. Tonight she was not Cindy the betrayed. She was Madame Destiny the magnificent. She couldn't let this man ruin her whole evening. She had never looked better. The new dress had lifted her beyond cuteness to exotic elegance. Actually, she realized, it was better that she found out this way rather than let herself be strung along and used. She probably had been saved from a broken heart and should thank him instead of being angry.

After this pep talk she felt a little better and threw herself wholeheartedly into having the time of her life. Her accent grew more dramatic and her actions more blatantly flirtatious. Madame Destiny had never been more provocative.

She picked at her meal, uninterested in the baked chicken entrée even if it hadn't been so difficult to eat with a veil. She remembered another night when she had satisfied her hunger by lifting her veil, but tonight she wouldn't dare take such freedoms. Besides, she had her mind on other matters.

Covertly she watched Nick and Felicia. Several times she caught his own gaze on her and wondered what he was thinking. Was he remembering her predictions or his evening with Cindy or their date, planned for the following day? She hoped he choked on his pastry swan.

As soon as the dishes had been cleared, the introductions were made. Cindy listened with a private smile of satisfaction at the swell of applause and wolf whistles that greeted Madame Destiny's introduction. Sitting back down, she noticed again that Nick was staring openly at her. Good!

After the introductions Preston went on to describe the accomplishments of the charity organization in the past year. Cindy tried to appear interested in his speech, but after the first few minutes her conscious mind tuned him out. In fact, not too many things penetrated her protective armor for the next hour as the speeches continued. It wasn't until the dancing started that she began enjoying herself. As soon as she stood up, she was

103

surrounded by men of all ages asking to be her partner on the dance floor. It was a phenomenon that had never happened to her before, and the attention quickly went to her head.

She didn't want to think about the fact that these men wouldn't have looked twice at Cindy Carroll. She forced herself to stop thinking about Nick and Felicia and kept her gaze from wandering among the other couples searching for them. Instead she turned the full force of Madame Destiny's considerable charms on her current partner and was rewarded by enough masculine attention to make the evening interesting.

Sparkling rays of lights reflected off the mirrored ball suspended from the ceiling. A live band provided a wide variety of music, and Cindy averaged three partners per song as they continued to cut in, never leaving her with one man for long. Fortunately most of them didn't ask her to answer any questions about their personal lives but just wanted to hold the slender, mysterious woman in their arms and try to catch a look at her well-guarded face or to hear her husky boudoir chuckle. They were trying to entertain her rather than the other way around.

"It looks like you're the belle of the ball," Preston observed with mixed feelings as he swept her across the floor. "I'm glad you're enjoying yourself, but this is the first time I've been able to get close enough to you to claim a dance. After all, I am your date."

"My escort," she corrected, "not my date." But she knew the petulant tone in his voice was all pretense and that he was as glad as she was that the evening was a success.

"That's what I get for 'escorting' the prettiest, most popular woman here."

"Excuse me, but may I cut in?" A prospective partner tapped Preston's shoulder.

"See? I told you so," Preston whispered to Cindy before stepping back and allowing the new man to take his place.

Cindy looked up and the smile slid from her face. "So, we meet again," she stated with a notable lack of enthusiasm.

"I'm amazed you remember me, and flattered." Nick observed her coolness, and after watching how vibrant she had been with her other partners, he couldn't help but wonder why she acted differently with him.

"I have a very good memory," she replied with a small shrug of dismissal.

Nick frowned, but he couldn't imagine what had brought on this sudden change in attitude. "I've been hoping I would have a chance to talk with you all evening."

"Oh, really? About what?" she asked in her best accent.

"I wanted to tell you that I did meet a woman in the coffee room last week, and I was hoping you'd be able to confirm that she's the one."

"Did you bring her with you tonight?" Cindy was proud of the detached indifference in her tone. She had no idea how she was managing to keep up this farce as she tried to follow his lead, especially since this was the first time she had ever danced with him. The light pressure of his hand on the small of her back was much too disturbing. But her masquerade was more important as she waited with hidden impatience for his answer.

"Good Lord, no. That's just Felicia."

Just Felicia? How she loved the implication of that.

"I wouldn't even be here tonight at all if she hadn't called me at the last minute and begged me to come with her. I felt a little bad about breaking up with her and I didn't have any other plans, so I agreed. If I had known you were going to be here, I wouldn't have hesitated."

"That's nice of you to say." Madame Destiny's voice warmed substantially after his explanation.

"I mean it. Like I told you before, I was all set to ignore your predictions, but you amazed me with your accuracy. When I met this really nice lady dressed in blue and wearing a weird ring, just like you said, well, I was astounded."

Cindy couldn't resist asking, "Do you like her?"

"A lot. I think I could fall in love with her very easily. We have a lot in common, laugh at the same jokes, and want the same things for the future."

"And your question to me was . . . ?"

"Is she my perfect mate? Or did I accidentally get sidetracked?"

"What would you do if I told you that she wasn't the one? Would you break it off with her and keep looking?"

Nick didn't hesitate. "No, I don't think so. I've only been on one date with her, and that wasn't even a real date, but she has everything I've ever wanted in a woman. She makes me feel like I can do anything I want to do and be anything I want to be. I haven't felt this way about myself or a woman since I was young."

"But would you have noticed her if I hadn't told you

about her?" No one but Cindy could ever know how important his answer to that question was.

"It's odd you should ask that. Apparently our paths have been crossing for over ten years and I had overlooked her until now. I can only blame that on the difference in our ages, which back then seemed a lot greater than it does now. But when I met her that day in the coffee room, she captured my interest immediately. I don't think my reaction to her would have been any different regardless of what you had said."

"So you're pleased with Madame Destiny?"

He could barely make out the features of her face beneath the veil. Her chocolate-brown eyes were heavily outlined in black, giving her an exotic look. Her complexion was very pale except for the dark hollows of her cheeks, but her smiling lips were a lively rose red. He wished he could get a better look at her. There was something about her that was vaguely familiar, but he couldn't place it. Of average height, she was slim and light in his arms. Surely he would never have forgotten a woman with such a spectacular figure.

"I'm very pleased with Madame Destiny *and* the new woman in my life."

"Don't forget to show your gratitude by making a donation to the charity."

Before Nick could answer, he felt a tap on his shoulder.

"May I cut in, please?"

"Sure," Nick replied, managing to give Madame Destiny a final smile and gently squeezing her hand before letting it go.

"Thanks again," he said before the new man stepped between them.

Cindy spent the rest of the evening dancing on air. Nick liked her a lot. He had said so in those exact words. And it sounded like he was planning to spend more time with her. He believed that she was his perfect mate, which made her ecstatically happy.

But along with all this joyful anticipation she couldn't help but be a little ashamed of herself. She should have told him who she really was, or at the very least not let him run on about her to her alter ego. Yet it had been such a relief to hear him say all those nice things about her and find out that Felicia was out of the picture. How long would she have had to date him before he would have told Cindy? She was sure the perfect time to reveal her harmless little masquerade would present itself and they would laugh together at how "destiny" had brought them together.

Cindy was ready when Nick arrived at her apartment the next day shortly after noon. She hoped he wouldn't guess that her wide, exuberant smile had nothing to do with the beautiful weather but with the relief and happiness brought on by his unwitting confession the night before. For the first time she felt completely relaxed with him. It was amazing how much it had meant to her to hear him say he really liked her. Not even trying to pretend an interest in the scenery, she kept her gaze focused on him as they talked. He drove with one hand on the wheel and one hand possessively holding hers as they crossed the James River and wound through the green countryside. She had no idea where they were going and didn't really care, as long as she was with Nick.

The flashy black sports car looked incongruous

against the stately backdrop of the Hickory Hill plantation. Located on the banks of the James River several miles northeast of Petersburg, the huge brick mansion was a page out of American history. It had been built in the mid-1700s on land that had been granted to its owners by King George I of England and had withstood the rigors of the Revolutionary War, the Civil War, and devastating attacks by the tax collectors and politicians of the Reconstruction. Still owned by descendants of the Latimer family, it had been opened to the public as a means of supporting itself.

Cindy and Nick took a self-guided tour of the beautifully restored building, except for the wing that had been set aside as a bed and breakfast.

"It's only a few miles from home, but I've always wanted to come here and spend a couple of days," Nick told her as they climbed the magnificent curving stairway up to the second floor.

"Yes, so would I," she answered as her hand slid along the polished oak banister. "It would be like stepping into a time capsule and going back to the days when life moved at a slower pace."

"It would be a good place for a honeymoon," Nick commented as they reached the landing and strolled into a large bedroom that was filled with exquisite antiques.

Cindy felt a blush creep up her neck and into her cheeks as her eyes followed his. An oversize four-poster bed, draped with a tatted canopy, dominated the room. It wasn't the implication that embarrassed her. It was just that her thoughts had been following the same line and it surprised her when he voiced them. It was as if he had read her mind, and in this genteel atmosphere it seemed an unladylike thing to be thinking about.

Together they wandered around the room, admiring the Queen Anne flat-top chest and matching desk. A crested silver brush-and-comb set were arranged on a mirrored tray on the dresser next to a framed, faded picture of a young girl who had just begun to show the promise of great beauty.

The windows offered an excellent view of the well-kept grounds that stretched for several hundred yards before sloping down to the river. Several barns and whitewashed corrals were visible to the left, and a group of slave cabins were almost hidden by a grove of oak trees to the right. It was easy to imagine the land bustling with people and animals working to keep the plantation alive.

At the end of their tour they stopped at the restaurant to pick up the picnic basket Nick had ordered, then strolled hand in hand across the emerald lawn. Though there were many visitors, they knew it wouldn't be difficult to find a nice private spot to eat.

Nick stopped by his car to get a blanket out of the trunk, then led her up a small hill. They spread the blanket beneath the ancient hickory trees from which the plantation had gotten its name and settled down to check out the contents of their basket.

"This is much nicer than eating inside and wasting a beautiful day like today," he commented as he glanced at the label approvingly before opening the bottle of wine that had been included.

Cindy set out their plates and silverware before unpacking a variety of cheeses and fruits, a loaf of French

110

bread, and two seafood salads. Southern-fried chicken and steaming corn on the cob completed the meal.

Nick poured the wine into the crystal goblets that had been in the basket and he lifted his in a toast. "To the lady destiny sent me."

Cindy was glad she didn't have anything in her mouth or she would have choked. Instead she managed a weak smile as their glasses touched. "To the Crimson Mystic," she added. Again their glasses touched, and they lifted them to their lips.

Though it had looked like a lot of food, they were both hungrier than they had thought and ate almost everything the restaurant had packed.

"I'm stuffed." Nick groaned, stretching out on his back in the shade. "I'll help you clean up in a minute. Why don't you come over here with me and we'll give all that good food a few minutes to settle?"

She didn't need a second invitation as she put the empty dishes she had been holding into the basket and crawled across the blanket until she was beside him. Lying on her stomach, she looked at his handsome face, knowing that she would never grow tired of seeing it. Without opening his eyes his arm wrapped around her waist and he pulled her over until her chest was resting on top of his.

"So tell me, Cindy. Did you miss me yesterday? I certainly missed you," he murmured, opening his eyes enough so he could watch her from beneath his half closed lids. "I hope you had a perfectly miserable time last night with the guy you turned me down for."

"Actually I had a wonderful time last night, but you have no reason to be jealous. I wasn't on a date. I had

111

promised to do something for someone, and I hated to back out at the last minute."

"Sick aunt? Visit to your grandmother? Your sister's wedding? Dirty bird cage?" he prompted, trying to get her to tell him about her evening as his other hand caressed the bare skin of her arm.

"None of those things," she said with a chuckle, "but it was a sort of goodwill expedition. Now, no more about my evening. What did you do last night?"

"I took an old friend to a dance—or rather she took me," he explained, waiting to see if she would show any of the signs of jealousy he would have felt if he had known she had gone out with another guy.

"So you finally found someone who didn't say no," she replied with a saucy tilt of her head. "I told you that you wouldn't have to spend your whole weekend working."

"I'll have you know that I didn't ask her *any* question that required a yes or no answer. The only person I want to hear a yes from is you." His fingers slid over her shoulder and buried themselves in the silken thickness of her hair.

"I've never told you no because you've never asked," she whispered as he pulled her closer.

"That's an oversight I'll soon correct." Rolling over until they were both lying on their sides, their bodies pressed together, they let their emotions do the talking.

Only the fact that they could be discovered at any moment kept them from going as far as their passions urged them. But their fervent kisses and increasingly bold caresses led them as close as they dared.

It was late in the afternoon when they finally replaced their leftovers in the basket, shook the grass and leaves from the blanket, and returned to the mansion. Nick's arm never relaxed its gentle hold on her as he turned in the basket and they walked to the car. Companionably, still basking in the glow of the first tender pangs of love, they took a long way home. Winding through the back roads of Virginia's Historic Triangle, they caught glimpses of other impressive plantation houses that had also been built along the river, and battlegrounds where thousands of soldiers had proven their courage and fought for their convictions.

Cindy alternated looking out the window with returning Nick's adoring glances. They were really much too wrapped up in each other to do justice to the beauty of the countryside. They still hadn't crossed back over the James River when the sun set and a full moon rose from behind the trees to bathe the landscape with a romantic glow.

"Is Kay going to be home tonight?" he asked after taking advantage of a stop sign to give Cindy a long, disturbing kiss.

"She had a rehearsal this evening, but she should be home by eight or nine."

"Damn. I wish I had a place of my own," Nick exclaimed, slapping the steering wheel with the palm of his hand. "I'm a grown man and I have no place to take you where we can be alone."

Cindy answered with a sympathetic sigh. She understood his distress because she, too, felt the sexual tension building between them. "Maybe we could just drive down by the river and look at the moon," she offered as a deceptively innocent solution.

He turned to face her with a rakishly crooked grin. "You mean go parking? I can't remember the last time I

113

went parking." At her answering smile he turned the car off the main road, following a narrow gravel lane until it dead-ended at the edge of the riverbank.

The moon did look spectacular, reflecting in a long, rippling strip on the river's dark waters, but Cindy and Nick didn't notice as they immediately melted into each other's arms. Surrounded by darkness and the throbbing hum of the locust, they resumed their lovemaking where they had left off earlier in the afternoon.

Nick adjusted her seat as far back as it would go, then he left his cramped position under the steering wheel to join her. The kisses he trailed along her cheek and down her neck were heated with desire. Cindy shifted beneath him, encouraging him without words. When his fingers moved to the buttons of her blouse, he hesitated, giving her time to say no, but her only response was to slide her hand under the bottom of his knit pullover shirt until her cool fingers stroked the bare skin of his back.

Surely she knew what she was doing to him . . . to his tenuous self-control. His desire and need for her had been mounting since their first kiss. With a moan he gave in to his feelings and quickly unbuttoned her blouse, pushing it aside so his hands could touch and his eyes could see her lovely body at last. Fumbling with her bra clasp, he finally succeeded in opening it and lifted it up to release her firm, full breasts.

The moonlight turned her skin to a milky alabaster, but instead of the cold smoothness of stone, her breasts were warm and soft in his hands.

"You're so beautiful," he breathed huskily, dropping a deep, hungry kiss on her lips before lowering his mouth to claim the rigid nipple that had hardened beneath the flicks of his thumb.

Cindy gasped as she felt the moistness of his mouth. His tongue circled and suckled until she almost burst with unfulfilled desire. Her fingers dug into the muscled flesh of his back, wanting him to keep on with this exquisite torture but also anxious for him to give her some relief.

"Lord, I want you," he whispered, lifting his head long enough to remove his shirt and help her slip out of her blouse and bra. "Damn, why did I buy a car with bucket seats and a stick shift on the console?" he grumbled as he tried to find a more comfortable position.

"Or at least a backseat," she added.

"I didn't think I would need one, especially not for this. Now I wish I had gotten a van or, better yet, an apartment. I'm getting too old for this sort of thing."

Cindy laughed at his dismay. It didn't matter to her as long as she was with Nick. Right now she was feeling totally decadent and wonderfully excited by being half naked with him on one of the bucket seats of his car.

They switched and adjusted their positions until they were half lying on her seat with their legs bent over the console and their feet on his seat. Their bare torsos pressed together as their lips met again and their hands conducted their own explorations.

Nick's hands lingered for a moment longer on the tempting delight of her breasts before moving down her rib cage and across her flat stomach to the waistband of her pants. Again the fastener challenged him, but soon he had eased the zipper down and touched the sensually silky material of her panties. His fingers slipped down until he found the object of his desires and could feel,

115

even through the thin barrier of cloth, that she was as ready to make love as he was.

She hadn't thought it possible for her to want a man this much, but she felt like she would die if he didn't take her now. Pushing her hips against his hand, her breasts flattened against the rough, dark hairs of his chest.

But it was crowded and muggy inside the car. Maybe they could take the blanket outside, she thought. But what if someone happened to go by on the river? The moon was bright enough that they would easily be seen. Besides, she noticed that a lightning storm had begun.

Nick's hands were pushing her pants down past her hips, and his mouth had discovered that sensitive spot on her neck that sent numbing tingles shooting down her arms.

The lightning was flashing steadily now, with almost no break between the strikes, she thought hazily. Beneath her heavy, half closed lids, her glazed eyes noticed that instead of being white, the flashes were red, then blue, then red, then—

"Oh, no," she cried, sitting up so abruptly that Nick tumbled backward. "It's the police!"

CHAPTER SEVEN

A moment of complete panic followed. Never had the interior of the sports car seemed smaller as Nick and Cindy tried to untangle their arms and legs and find their clothes. Cindy's shirt was nowhere to be seen, and as a last resort Nick helped her slip into his while she struggled to refasten the waist of her pants. And still the red-and-blue lights from the patrol car rotated, sending their colors bouncing off the windows and mirrors like a laser show.

"You kids havin' a good time?" a gruff baritone voice asked outside Nick's window seconds before a flashlight was clicked on and shined in at the occupants.

Temporarily blinded, Cindy and Nick blinked and tried to look as nonchalant as possible.

"Well, what have we here?" The policeman's tone now held a hint of laughter as he bent down and peered into the low-slung vehicle. "Do your mothers know what you're doing?" he asked, no longer holding back a snicker.

"Is there a problem, Officer?" Nick asked as casually as a half-naked man could.

"Yes, I'd say there was. For openers, you're trespassing on private property."

117

"Oh, we didn't know." Nick was acutely uncomfortable and could feel his cheeks burning with embarrassment. Certain that Cindy must be as humiliated as he was, he clasped her slim hand in his for comfort.

"We got a complaint that some parkers were blocking a driveway. Somehow you aren't what I was expecting to find. Aren't you a little old for this?" The patrolman turned the glaring beam of his flashlight on Cindy, who hadn't made a sound. Immediately the officer's voice hardened. "How about you, miss? If you're underage, this man could be in a lot of trouble."

"B-but—" Nick sputtered, turning to Cindy. In her disheveled state with her reddish-blond hair wildly tousled, her full lips looking swollen and pouty from all his kisses, and dressed in his oversize shirt, she did look very young. Shaking his head, he shut his mouth and waited after the officer requested identification and Cindy found her purse, then pulled out her driver's license.

With narrowed eyes, the patrolman read, "June 14, 1962. You're going to be twenty-five next week?" At Cindy's nod he swept his light over her again, and still looking a little doubtful, he turned his attention back to Nick. "I'm going to let the two of you off with a warning this time, but don't let me catch you out here again. Loitering is illegal. Parking could be very dangerous, and you can interpret that advice any way you want." Hitching his belt up, the officer turned and walked back to his patrol car, calling to his partner, "It's just a couple of over-the-hill teenagers. You should see the way they're dressed." The sound of his laughter carried through the windless night.

Nick reached over and recaptured Cindy's hand. "I

can't believe it. To be caught parking at my age—and with you. At least we're far enough from Petersburg that we shouldn't ever meet that county sheriff again. It would have been even more embarrassing if it had been someone from our hometown that knew one or both of us. Lord, I just can't believe it," he repeated dismally. He felt Cindy's hand begin to tremble in his, and he turned to her with words of reassurance on his lips. She must be very upset by this whole experience.

"Please don't be frightened," he continued gently. "It was all my fault. I should have been more careful. I should never have—" His apologies broke off as he realized that she was not shaking because she was upset but because she was laughing.

"He actually asked for my ID. He thought you were trying to take advantage of a minor," she said. "We look so ridiculous with me wearing your shirt and you without one and our hair all messed up. I thought I was going to laugh out loud while he was here and get us both arrested."

"You think this is funny?"

"Yes, I think it's hilarious. Did you see the look on his face when he realized you weren't a kid?" She leaned back in her seat and held her stomach as she laughed again.

He stared at her incredulously for another few seconds, then laughed with her. It wasn't until the patrol car behind them punched his siren that they were reminded of where they were. Obediently Nick started his engine and drove forward until he found a place large enough to turn around.

"I didn't notice that this road led to a house, did

you?" he asked as he traveled back along the gravel lane with the police car following.

"No, I was too busy looking at the moon."

"Having a cop shine a flashlight in your face is more sobering than a cold shower," Nick commented wryly as he drove onto the highway headed for Petersburg.

"I'd better find the rest of my clothes before we get back into town. This is something I'd rather not have to explain."

She searched around the car until she found her bra and blouse stuffed into the space between her seat and her door, then went through a series of contortions while getting redressed without actually having to take his shirt off until she was through.

"Here," she said brightly as she handed him his shirt and refastened her seat belt. "Thanks a lot."

"I would say anytime, but I don't plan on having this happen again. Either we're going to have to find a place of our own or stop letting ourselves get so carried away."

It turned out to be the latter as a new week began. Nick, still unsure of how the other employees would react to the news, talked it over with Cindy, and they decided that it would be best to keep their budding relationship at a low profile at the office. As it turned out, she was still too busy trying to run the personnel department to spend much time romancing the boss, anyway.

Her secretary was back, but Don was not, so she still had to handle both jobs. Fortunately she wouldn't have to deal with the copy machine or the coffeepot, even though she held no grudges against the two machines. After all, they had helped bring her and Nick together.

In spite of the baffled curiosity of his secretary, Nick managed to find endless excuses to pay visits to the personnel department every day. However, he and Cindy made it a point not to meet in the coffee room for fear that someone might overhear a careless word spoken by one of the moonstruck lovers. As promised, he had put out a memo so that the male employees would make their share of the coffee, which took away her excuse for being there so often.

Instead, every afternoon when she was finally able to get away from her office, Cindy jumped into her car with its shiny new battery and hurried home to her apartment. Usually Nick would meet her there later and they would either go out to eat or stay there and fix something together. If Kay wasn't busy, she would sometimes join them on these informal dates, but she always conscientiously disappeared toward the end of the evening so Nick and Cindy would have some time alone.

But they had learned the hard way the consequences of going too far, and they tried to keep their emotions in control. That didn't mean they didn't spend most of their private time together kissing and caressing each other, but knowing they would have to stop kept them from getting carried away.

Friday afternoon Cindy had just finished the week's insurance claims and given them to her secretary for copying when Nick rushed into her office.

"Do you have time to come with me to the back for a few minutes?" he asked, his face glowing with excitement.

Though she didn't have the faintest idea what he had

121

in mind, she didn't hesitate and quickly locked her office.

"Where are you taking me? Have you found a new parking spot?" she teased, keeping her voice low.

"Hush before I tell everyone how *cute* you look in my shirt," he whispered back.

They hurried across the reception area and down the hallway that divided the offices into departmental sections. He held the heavy metal door that separated the factory from the offices open for her, then followed her into the cavernous work area where all of the company's products were made and packaged. It was not the type of manufacturing that required hard hats, but many of the employees had to wear goggles and ear protectors when operating the machinery.

Again Nick took the lead as they walked through the maze of equipment, both of them answering greetings from the workers as they passed through. The machines roared and clattered as some of them poured liquid plastics into the pen-barrel molds, while others cut the small tubing of the cartridges that were then fastened to the ballpoints or felt tips before being filled with ink. Everything was mechanized, but because of the many different styles and colors of the barrels and inks, a lot of human supervision was required.

They walked the entire length of the production line until they reached the end where the finished products were either sealed in blister packs or put in boxes to be stored in the warehouse until shipment.

"It's almost ready, Mr. Wainwright. It should be coming off the line any second now," one of the workers called to Nick when he saw them approaching.

"Hurry up, Cindy. We don't want to miss this." Not

caring what anyone thought, Nick grabbed her hand and pulled her along until they stood beside a small group of factory employees. A little breathless from the briskness of their walk and the excitement, they waited.

"What are we waiting for?" Cindy asked in a natural voice that, considering the noise in the room, sounded more like a whisper. She looked from one expectant face to another, wondering why they were all staring at the wide, moving belt that should have had a pen in each ridge in the last stage of the assembly line. Instead the belt kept rolling through its endless circles with nothing on its black rubber surface.

"Look, here it comes now."

All eyes focused on a gold-colored pen that nestled in its little slot as it moved toward them. Nick reached out and picked it up before it could travel on to the packing belt.

"Here it is. The first of my own creations, fresh off the line. What do you think?" Almost reverently he handed it to Cindy and waited for her reaction.

She looked at its slim, sleek design, but it was the unique triangular shape that caught her eye. Settling the pen between her thumb and fingers, as if she were writing, she could see why Nick was so excited.

"It's brilliant, Nick. Look how perfectly it fits into the natural grip. I'll bet it will cut down on sore fingers and cramping from a lot of writing."

"That's the whole idea," Nick said, pleased that she understood his plan so quickly. "This is the prototype for a new style that I plan on naming the Easy Writer. We're going to put it out in both felt tip and ballpoint and in multiple colors. I'm hoping it will set our competition on their ears . . . or maybe their inkwells." He paused for effect before adding, "See? I told you I was working last weekend."

"No one has ever accused you of being a slow worker," she commented with a knowing twinkle in her hazel eyes.

He responded with a confidential wink at her, then turned to the other workers. "How did it go? Was it very complicated to adapt our machinery to this new design?"

"No, it just took a few minor adjustments. As soon as you give the go-ahead, we'll turn over the entire number twelve production line and start rolling out thousands a day."

"Good. Let me give it a final check and I'll get back to you. Meanwhile let's get started on that order of colored markers to be shipped to Texas. And thanks, guys. You did a great job." Motioning for Cindy to follow, he left the factory and returned to her office. Taking the pen from her, he picked up her notepad and drew the outline of a heart, then wrote "Nick & Cindy" in its center. "How's that?" he asked proudly.

"Are you asking about the way the pen works or what you wrote?"

"Let's start with the pen. We'll talk about the other later."

"Here, let me try it." Positioning the pen in her hand, she drew a large arrow through the center and made a squiggly, lacelike border around the outside of the heart. "It's smooth and comfortable. I really like it. But how did you come up with the idea?"

"Have you ever seen those little rubber triangles that slip over the ends of pencils called grippers? Elementary-school children use them to help them learn how to correctly hold and control their pencils. I just adapted that idea into a molded pen shape."

"I think it will be a huge success."

"I hope so. It will be my first chance to show that I have what it takes to run this company. I'll feel like I've really contributed to the success of Wainwright Ink."

"You're doing a fine job," she reassured him sincerely.

"Now, let's talk about the other," he whispered, moving up behind her and nibbling on her earlobe. "Have I told you that I think I've fallen in love with you?"

"No. Tell me," she breathed, leaning her head back against his shoulder.

"You're so good for me. You make me feel like I'm someone important."

"You *are* important. Especially to me."

He turned her in his arms until she was facing him. "Not as important as you are to me, pretty lady." His lips had just grazed hers when a loud knock interrupted them.

"Miss Carroll, are you in there? I'm finished with the insurance files."

"It's my secretary," Cindy whispered as they sprang apart.

"The whole world is conspiring against us." He sighed in resignation. "Tonight we'll celebrate the Easy Writer and maybe find some time to continue this conversation too."

"Don't forget that we're supposed to go to the play. It's opening night, and Kay has gotten us some good tickets."

He nodded and picked up his pen, letting Cindy's secretary in as he left. It looked like he was going to have to marry his destiny's lady if he ever wanted to have any time alone with her.

"So when are you going to tell him about Madame Destiny?" Kay asked that evening as they were getting ready for their dates. Nick was going to bring a friend of his along for Kay, and they were all going out together after the play.

"As soon as I'm sure he loves me enough to understand. Today he told me he thinks he loves me, but I want to wait until he is absolutely certain."

"You still don't feel secure enough to tell him?"

"I still can't believe we're together, much less feel secure with our relationship," Cindy cried. "I want to tell him, but I just can't. Not yet." She was beginning to lose count of how many times she had said that in the last couple of weeks. But she was too afraid to take a chance of losing him. She had even begun to consider the possibility of turning over Madame Destiny's dress to someone new and keeping the secret forever. But honesty was too much a part of her character to seriously think of that as an alternative. No, she must bide her time and keep her secret until she knew Nick wouldn't be upset.

Kay had to stay backstage during the entire play, but Cindy, Nick, and Mike, Kay's date, watched from their third-row seats, enjoying the music, the costumes, and the surprisingly good acting of the small ensemble group. They waited for Kay after the show, and then the entire group proceeded to Brandy's, a trendy new restaurant in a local hotel.

"This is not what I call being alone," Nick shouted to be heard above the noise of the exuberant crowd. "This is almost as bad as trying to talk in the factory. How soon can we politely leave?"

"Not until Kay is ready. This is her celebration. She's worked so hard on that play that I owe it to her, as her best friend, to stay for a while."

"We are at a hotel." He leaned closer until he was speaking directly into her ear. "I could get us a room and we could slip away."

The tip of his tongue followed the curve of her ear, and his warm breath was like a physical caress. She felt her already weakened resistance fade away completely. "Hmm, maybe that would be all right. I'm sure Kay would understand."

A tingle of anticipation swept through Nick's body. Tonight he would be able to hold Cindy in his arms as long as he wanted, to kiss her delicious lips and touch her beautiful body, to please her and satisfy himself all night long. He nearly knocked his chair over in his haste to get up. "I'll be right back, my love. I promise this will be a night to remember."

Cindy wasn't sure what she should be feeling, but as she watched his trim, athletic body maneuver through the crowd with moves that would have made any quarterback proud, she wondered why she wasn't more excited at the prospect of spending the night with Nick. She wanted to make love with him. After all, this dream might end at any time, and she wanted to have as much of Nick as she could get. She wanted to fall asleep next to him and wake up to his kisses. She wanted to make enough memories to last the rest of her life in case he didn't fall in love with her. Why, then, wasn't her pulse racing and her heart pounding?

Instead she was feeling a little disappointed. Some-

how she had always thought that their first night together would be romantic and spontaneous. All this
premeditation and planning took something special out
of it. In the front seat of his car it had been the heat of
the moment that would have kept it from being tawdry,
but this seemed so coldly calculated.

Nick's long strides took him quickly across the lobby
to the registration desk.

"I'd like a double room, please," he said, pulling his
wallet out of his hip pocket.

"I'm sorry, sir, but we're all booked up. Except"—
the pretty clerk punched a code into her computer and
smiled at Nick—"the bridal suite is open. It's a bit more
expensive than our normal double rooms, but it's quite
nice. Would you like me to book that for you?"

Nick found himself in a real dilemma. He wanted
Cindy so much, it hurt. His body ached to possess her,
and he knew she felt the same way. But did he want to
turn their romance into an affair? Then again, would he
kick himself tomorrow if he turned down what appeared to be their best opportunity to be truly alone for
any time in the near future?

Damn, why hadn't they had any room available except the bridal suite? He couldn't take Cindy to the
bridal suite until they were truly married.

It came as quite a revelation, but he *did* want to
marry her. And he wanted it to be perfect and beautiful,
not some quickie in a hotel room.

"Sir?"

"Oh, I'm sorry. But no, thanks. I don't think I'll need
a room tonight, after all." With that he spun on his
heels and returned to the restaurant. It was amazing
that being forced into all those decisions had had the

same cooling effect on him as being confronted by a policeman on a dark, deserted country road. By the time he got back to their table, he had begun to wonder how he was going to explain this sudden change of heart to Cindy. Would she be terribly disappointed? Would she think he no longer found her desirable? Lord, he thought, falling in love sure made his life more complicated.

"Hi," he said. He knew his smile was a little too stiff, but he couldn't help it.

"Hi, yourself," she bantered back, looking at him curiously. He was acting much differently than when he had left. His brilliant blue eyes were no longer burning with passion or his voice trembling with desire. This was going to be worse than she had imagined. How was she going to break it to him that she had changed her mind?

"Cindy—"

"Nick—"

They both began together and stopped at the same time.

"I didn't get—"

"I don't want—"

Again they started and stopped at the same instant. They shared a nervous laugh. To keep it from happening a third time Nick reached out and placed his fingers lightly against her lips.

"Shh. Let's go over to the atrium where we can talk," he said as he took his hand away from her mouth and held it out for her.

She took it and let him pull her up and lead her away from most of the noise.

"Cindy," he began again. "I just realized how much I love you."

"It just came to you in a flash while you were in the lobby?" she asked incredulously.

"Sort of. I started falling in love with you the first time we talked together in the coffee room, but I didn't know how much until a few minutes ago.

"First of all," he continued, "I want you to know that there's nothing I want more than for us to spend the night together. Lord, that's all I can think about twenty hours a day."

"What about the other four?"

"That's when I'm thinking about all the good reasons why we should wait. And when I was in the lobby, I guess I used up part of that time by deciding that I love you too much to rent a hotel room just so we can make love. Our relationship just isn't like that, and I don't think we should turn it into that. Do you understand?"

"Oh, Nick," she cried, tears filling her eyes, making them sparkle like emeralds floating in gold dust. "You are the most wonderful man in the world. I love you so much."

"Then you're not disappointed?"

"Sure, I'm disappointed. But I had already made up my mind that tonight . . . like that . . . it just wasn't the right thing for us. I was afraid you'd be mad at me and think I had been teasing you."

He reached out and pulled her into his arms. "I know you better than that. You're no tease. You're the most honest person I know. That's one of the reasons I fell in love with you."

Cindy was sobbing in earnest now. She wasn't as honest and noble as he made it sound. She had lied to him.

She had practically pushed herself on him. She had even deceived him a second time at the ball. It didn't matter that she hadn't done these things maliciously or that it had been a spur-of-the-moment action. If she told him now, it would tarnish his image of her forever. And she loved him so much that she couldn't bear to lose him.

"Don't cry, honey," he murmured soothingly. His hand pushed a silken strand of her hair back from her face, and he wiped the tears from beneath her eyes with the tip of a forefinger. "We've got the rest of our lives to be together."

CHAPTER EIGHT

Kay and Mike had hit it off so well that the four friends decided to double-date the next evening. They had to wait until Kay helped the theater group get their makeup on and start the play, but it wasn't necessary for her to stay for the finish.

On the drive into Richmond for dinner they tried to think of a nice place that allowed their semi-casual dress. Everyone had their favorite spot, but they finally settled on the Traveller's Restaurant.

"I agree that they have good food, but there's something strange about eating in a place that used to be a stable and is named after a horse," Mike protested good-naturedly.

"That's part of its charm," Kay replied. "You can tell your grandchildren that you ate in the same place that General Robert E. Lee's horse did."

Everyone laughed and began adding comments of their own until the history of Richmond and its famous residents would never be the same again. In the backseat Nick and Cindy had the advantage of being able to cuddle during the half-hour trip. They had decided to ride in Mike's car because Nick's didn't have enough room.

After an excellent steak dinner the couples tried to get a little exercise by walking through the Sixth Street Marketplace. But even after lingering at many of the specialty shops the evening was still much too young for them to head for home.

"Where do you guys want to go now? You name it and I'll take you there," Mike volunteered.

"Hawaii would be nice," Nick suggested.

"I've always wanted to see the Grand Canyon," Cindy chimed in.

"How about the Statue of Liberty? I haven't seen her since she got her face-lift," Kay added.

"Comedians! I'm the only sane person in a car full of comedians," Mike said with a groan. "Okay. You've just relinquished your rights to choose. From now on it's driver's choice. Hang on because you are fixing to see Richmond by night."

Unless there was traffic or a red light, Mike barely slowed down as they took a fast tour of the city. They zipped around the Virginia State Capitol, which had been designed by Thomas Jefferson, and the nearby Governor's Mansion. They drove down Monument Avenue, which was supposed to be one of the most beautiful thoroughfares in America, although it was too dark to appreciate any of the handsome old houses. And no one argued when Mike didn't stay at the Edgewood house long enough to catch sight of the ghost of Elizabeth Rowland, who, it was rumored, was still, after more than a hundred years, searching for her lover, who hadn't come home from the war.

Finally they found themselves heading out of town to the Richmond-Petersburg Turnpike. It wasn't until they

133

passed the Virginia State Fairgrounds that Mike was inspired to stop.

"Hey, when's the last time any of you guys have been to an old-fashioned carnival?" he asked enthusiastically.

"Funny you should ask, because it hasn't been but about two weeks," Nick answered. "Didn't anyone else in this car go to the charity carnival the Saturday before last?"

"Did it have a Ferris wheel or a Bullet?" At Nick's negative answer Mike stated emphatically, "Then it didn't count. A *real* carnival has to have at least five sickening rides or it's a cheap imitation. How about you ladies? Do you want to be sticks-in-the-mud or do you want to be wild and impulsive and have a lot of fun?"

"I haven't been to a carnival since high school. Remember, Cindy? We used to go to the state fair every year," Kay said. "We used to have a great time blowing our money on those games, trying to win a stuffed animal."

"Which we never won," Cindy said with a smile. "For what we spent trying, we could have bought enough stuffed animals to start our own booth."

"But it wouldn't have been the same," her friend replied.

By mutual consent Mike made a U-turn at the first exit and went back to the fairgrounds.

"The state fair is always in the fall, so this must be some sort of traveling carnival," Mike said as he parked the car and everyone began getting out.

"Maybe the charity is putting this on. I'm sure it would be a bigger production since it's in a bigger town," Nick stated with mounting excitement.

"Why this sudden preoccupation with charities?

Have you suddenly turned philanthropic in your old age?" Mike cast a puzzled look at his friend as they started walking toward the colorful midway.

"It's a good cause, but that's not the only reason. It sounds a little silly, but I met this fortune-teller on two different occasions, and she told me some pretty amazing things about myself. Anyway, I've been wanting to introduce Cindy to her. I hope she's here tonight."

Kay gave Cindy a knowing look, and Cindy responded with a helpless shrug.

They bought a handful of tickets at a small booth, then headed toward the rides. At this time of the evening the crowds had begun to thin, so there were almost no lines on even the most popular rides. It took them less than an hour to turn a strange shade of green.

"I don't remember ever feeling this way after riding on a Tilt-a-Whirl. Lord, I used to ride it a dozen times consecutively after eating a couple of greasy chili dogs and still be hungry for onion rings." Nick was sitting on a wooden bench next to Cindy and leaning his head on her shoulder, wishing fervently that the world would stop spinning.

"Please don't talk about food right now." Mike groaned, slouching forward and resting his face in his hands.

"I haven't been able to swallow properly since the Scrambler," Cindy added, her arms crossed over her stomach.

"I think it was the merry-go-round that got me." Kay fanned her face with her hand, hoping the night air would make her feel better.

The other three turned, and they managed to focus

their attention on Kay long enough to give her quizzical looks.

"Well, it did," she insisted. "It was all that round-and-round and up-and-down."

All four of them moaned simultaneously and fell back into their limp positions.

"It hurts to admit it, but this must be a sign of old age. There wasn't a ride in the world that would make me feel nauseous when I was younger. I'd hate to think what would happen to me if I got on a roller coaster now," Nick said, grumbling.

"Speaking of old age, are you planning on going to the reunion next Saturday?" Mike asked, his voice muffled by his fingers. "I think most of our classmates are going to be there. I can't believe it's been ten years since graduation from good ol' PHS."

"Neither can I," Nick replied. "And no, I haven't decided whether or not to go. I'd like to see everybody again, but I'm afraid if I go back, I'll relive one game too many and ruin my memories."

"Well, I'm going if I live through tonight, and I plan on asking Kay to go with me. Maybe we could double again."

Nick didn't commit himself, and several minutes of silence passed before anyone felt recuperated enough to leave the bench and explore the rest of the carnival.

"I've still got some tickets left." Mike held up the string of colored paper.

"Me too. But I don't want to try any more rides. What are we going to do with them?" asked Nick.

"We could give them away."

"Or throw them away."

"There's a fun house," Cindy pointed out. "That sounds pretty tame. What about it?"

They pushed through a pair of doors and found themselves in a maze of mirrored walls. Kay and Mike took the lead and soon disappeared around a corner. Nick and Cindy had been making faces at each other in the mirrors and hadn't seen which way they had gone. Trying to catch up with them, they turned in the wrong direction and found themselves squeezed into a narrow dead end.

Cindy bumped into the wall first, then immediately turned to head in the opposite direction. Nick, who was following close behind her, didn't have time to stop, and they collided. Automatically his arms reached out to steady her. Looking up into his laughing eyes, surrounded by millions of reflections of themselves, she again marveled at how lucky she was, and how wonderfully happy.

She could feel the coldness of the glass behind her back and hear the screams and laughter of other people who were also lost in the maze, echoing through the small room although she and Nick were quite alone. It was a strange moment, like they had fallen into an unreal world. Her arms slipped around his waist and her body pressed against his warmth.

"Have I told you today that I love you?" he asked with a sexy, crooked grin.

"Yes, you have, but I wouldn't mind hearing it again and again and again." Her words were silenced by his kiss, as light and gentle as the brush of a butterfly's wings, first on her lips, then on each of her closed eyelids. His hand wrapped around the back of her neck, supporting the weight of her head as his mouth returned to her lips for a lazy, sensual kiss.

"There you are, hiding in the—whoops. Did we interrupt something?" Mike asked as he and Kay joined them in the narrow chamber.

"I'm beginning to get claustrophobic," Nick muttered, his lips moving against hers. His broad shoulders were pressed against each wall so he couldn't turn around. "Hey, you guys. Move back so we can get out of here." Rolling his eyes at Cindy, he managed a resigned smile as he backed out of the tiny room and into the main passageway.

"Here I thought we had outsmarted the two of you by beating you through the maze, when all the time you were lost on purpose," Mike said, teasing them as he led the way around several corners, cutting back and forth until they entered a large room. Four full-length mirrors stood directly in front of them, giving each a wildly distorted view of themselves.

"Now I know how it feels to be tall." Cindy laughed at her lengthened image, then looked over at Nick's squatty reflection. "Hello, shorty. How do you like dating a woman that's taller than you?"

"I think tall women are intimidating. I'd rather fall in love with a short, cute woman any day," he answered.

"How about a short, fat woman?" Cindy asked, moving over next to Kay, whose mirror made them look as wide as they were tall. They all switched places, posing and laughing until a group of teenagers stumbled out of the maze behind them.

They walked as quickly as possible across a rickety bridge and through a constantly revolving barrel that was barely tall enough to keep Nick from bumping his head.

"Hey, remember when we used to do this?" Nick called to Mike, and the others turned around to watch Nick brace his hands on the ceiling, spread his legs, and remain in a standing position as the barrel slowly rolled him upside down.

"Show-off," Mike said, taunting him. "You'll regret that later."

Nick waited until he had returned to an upright position, then staggered out to join them. "I don't have to wait until later. I regret it already."

"I was very impressed," Cindy said, reassuring him extravagantly and patting his arm. "I've never had a man fall head over heels for me before."

"Well, you have now," he whispered in her ear.

Nick insisted on checking out all the booths and was mildly disappointed to find that the only fortune-teller on the premises was Mother Lucy. As far as he was concerned, Madame Destiny was one of a kind.

"Maybe I could get her phone number from someone at the charity and ask her to set up a booth at the company's Fourth of July picnic," he suggested casually, and was startled by the vehement response from both Cindy and Kay.

"No! Absolutely not," the two women said almost simultaneously, then exchanged stricken looks.

"What's the matter with you two? Neither of you have even met her. I think you'd be quite impressed."

"Oh, it isn't that," Kay hastened to add, trying to cover for her friend. "It's just that you said she only works for charity, so I'm sure she wouldn't be interested in a private affair."

Cindy cringed at the unfortunate choice of words and waited for Nick's response.

"Oh, I wouldn't mind donating a generous sum to cover her time."

Drastic events called for drastic measures, and Cindy decided it was time to dissuade him from this absurd idea before it went too far. "Nick, you really should wait until you've known the employees and their habits better before you start changing traditions about the company picnic. I think they prefer to spend the day with their families, eating, drinking, and playing. Surely you remember going with your father when you were younger. Everyone just wants to relax and have some plain old country fun. Madame Destiny just wouldn't fit into that atmosphere."

"I guess you're right." He nodded reluctantly, then brightened. "Maybe we can get her for the Christmas dance. That would be even better."

"Nick, I'm becoming a little jealous of her," Cindy said, pretending to pout. "You talk about her more than you talk about me."

"With her I talk. With you I make love," he murmured, dropping a kiss on the top of her red-gold hair. "You, my pretty lady, have nothing and no one to be jealous about," he stated firmly.

Cindy yawned and stretched, not really ready to wake up but knowing that if she didn't, she would be late to church. Slowly, one limb at a time, she eased out of bed. She felt groggy, almost like she had a hangover, but they hadn't even had any wine with dinner the night before. It must be residual vertigo from the carnival rides or Nick's amorous embraces on the trip home, she decided.

Something was wrapped around her right ankle, and she couldn't seem to pull her leg across the bed. The thing was soft, furry, and alarming. Pushing the covers down, she laughed with relief when she saw the cause of her difficulties. Tangled in her sheet was a snake, bright yellow with a felt forked tongue and round black eyes. Reaching down, she untangled it from the covers and her ankle and hugged it to her chest.

Nick had won it by throwing footballs through a tire. The twelve consecutive bull's-eyes had cost him only a dollar. His skill had come as no surprise to Cindy, because she knew the Crimson Mystic had always been able to peg a fly in midair with one of his passes. Even after all those years he still had it . . . and she still wanted it.

Cindy finally stumbled from her room and headed toward the kitchen and a cup of coffee that would hopefully help clear her head. Kay was already in there, shaking two aspirin out of the bottle as she impatiently waited for the coffee to finish brewing.

"Give me a couple of those, too, please." Cindy took a mug out of the cabinet and joined Kay by the coffee maker.

"Happy Birthday," Kay said with a shaky smile after she had poured them both a cup of freshly brewed coffee. They clicked their mugs together, tossed the aspirin in their mouths, and completed their salute with a sip of coffee.

"Thanks. I'd almost forgotten that today was my birthday."

"It does get pretty forgettable after your twenty-first,

doesn't it? Oh, by the way, there's a florist's box over on the table that was delivered for you this morning."

"For me?" she repeated in surprise. "I didn't even hear the door bell."

"I wouldn't have if I hadn't been on my way to the medicine cabinet. Well, hurry up and open it. I'm dying to see who it's from—as if I didn't already know."

Cindy slid the satin ribbon off the long white box and lifted off the lid. Nestled in a ruffled layer of tissue paper was a gardenful of yellow roses.

"Gosh," Kay gasped. "How many are in there? It must be two or three dozen."

Cindy gathered them into her arms and held them up so she could bury her face in their fragrant blossoms. The delicate petals were soft against her cheeks. "They're beautiful, aren't they? I don't think we have a vase large enough for them, though."

"Don't worry about that. We'll put them in the aquarium if we have to. The fish would probably enjoy a change of scenery. They'll think we've sent them to the Sequoia National Forest on a vacation. Look, here's the card."

Cindy gently returned the flowers to their box and picked up the small pink envelope. She removed the card and silently read the scrawled note.

"Happy birthday dearest Cindy. I'm sorry I can't be with you today, but something important has come up. I'll meet you at your parents' house about seven and promise to be on my best behavior. Love, love, love, Nick. P.S. This was written with my Easy Writer. Looks terrific, doesn't it?"

When she and Kay got back from church, the apart-

142

ment smelled like someone had sprayed a whole can of rose-scented air freshener in there.

"Whew. It's a little overpowering, isn't it?" Cindy said understating a bit.

"But they are impressive." Kay chuckled. "I wish I had a boyfriend who would send me even a single rose."

"I noticed you and Mike were pretty chummy last night. Is he a maybe?"

"Maybe!"

They quickly changed their clothes and went to Cindy's parents' house where they had been invited for dinner and a family birthday celebration.

Nick was a nervous wreck when he finally met Cindy's parents. He hadn't been that fidgety since the last time he had played in the Cotton Bowl. But with Cindy's hand firmly clasped in his, he met the people he hoped would someday become his in-laws.

"So how does it feel to be a quarter of a century old?" he asked later when they were sitting in the backyard, cuddling on the porch swing.

"You should know, old man. You're getting pretty close to the big three-oh, aren't you?"

"Thanks for reminding me. But you've only got five years left before you'll be there too."

"Is this how you cheer a woman up?"

"I can't help it. I feel especially old this month. There's my ten-year reunion next week, and I've fallen in love with an almost old woman."

Cindy nibbled on her lower lip and frowned. "Are you going to your reunion?"

Nick shrugged. "I guess so. Everyone keeps telling me I'll kick myself if I miss it. And after all, it only comes around once every ten years."

143

"Oh," she whispered. So the conquering hero was going to return to his field of glory, she thought. Surrounded by cheerleaders and old girlfriends, it would be a miracle if he even remembered her name by the end of the evening. Just when she had begun to relax and feel a little comfortable with their relationship, this darn reunion had to come up. Her insecurities swept through her, taking away the evening's pleasure. Cindy knew she was being paranoid, but she couldn't help it.

"You will go with me, won't you?" he asked, misunderstanding her sudden stiffness by thinking she was afraid she would be uncomfortable with all those strangers. "You already know a few of my friends, and Kay might go with Mike, so you wouldn't feel totally left out. I promise not to leave you alone."

She nodded, feeling somewhat relieved that at least she would be there to witness the seduction. Between now and then, maybe she would be able to sharpen her claws a little so she could protect her interests.

But still she worried about it for the next six days. Nick continued being as sweet and attentive as he had been before, but she could sense a growing excitement within him as the big day approached. As he went from indifference to anticipation Cindy's spirits drooped. It hadn't helped that Don had called in and requested another week off, leaving her in charge. But it had been an especially busy week since the Easy Writer had gone into production and five new employees had to be hired to handle the extra workload.

Saturday night she and Nick arrived at the hotel promptly at six o'clock, and Cindy nervously smoothed the skirt of her new emerald-green silk cocktail dress on which she had splurged almost half a week's salary. The money would be well spent if it helped her get through this evening with even a shred of self-confidence. Even after all these years she felt intimidated at the prospect of spending so much time with people who had been her upperclassmen.

As they walked into the same ballroom where the ball had been held, Nick commented, "Aren't there any other hotels in this town that can handle a crowd? I've only been back for about seven months, and of all the parties I've been to, this is the third one that has been held here."

"It's a very nice hotel," Cindy replied absently. She, too, had been a little surprised at the coincidence, but right now that was the least of her worries.

The ballroom had WELCOME CLASS OF '77 signs hung on the walls, and the whole room had been decorated to look like a pep rally. Red and gold streamers were draped around the walls and met in a fluffy ball in the middle at the crystal chandelier. Hundreds of red helium-filled balloons bumped up against the ceiling, with curling ribbons hanging down from them to just above the people's heads. A display with a montage of old snapshots, spirit ribbons, and copies of the school newspaper dominated one corner of the room, while a private deejay had set up his stereo system at the other end.

Cindy pinned a name tag to her dress, hoping it wouldn't permanently damage the material. She also hoped that Nick wouldn't notice that the plain, bespectacled little girl in one of the old pictures was not nearly as attractive as some of the other women that would be here tonight.

There weren't many people there yet, and most of

them seemed more interested in checking out the bar than greeting new arrivals. But as soon as she and Nick walked into the ballroom, a crowd formed around him. Cindy knew he had been very popular and had been expecting this. After the first few awkward moments, through which Nick had kept his arm protectively draped around her shoulders and had thoughtfully introduced her and kept her involved in the conversation, she began to relax. She was surprised at how many people she either remembered or had met since graduation through her work or social life.

By the time Kay and Mike arrived, Mike having decided to take his own car, Cindy was already beginning to enjoy herself. It was fun seeing these people, ten years older, and finding out what they had done with their lives. Several of the men were already beginning to go bald, and quite a few of the women had lost their slender figures somewhere between childbirth and sitting at a desk all day. Secretly Cindy breathed a little easier when she noticed that most of the cheerleaders no longer resembled their pictures, either.

It was amazing what an equalizer ten years was.

She was proud to be with Nick, and he made it very obvious to everyone that he was proud to be with her. Even on the dance floor it was with the greatest reluctance that he let anyone cut in. He was charmingly possessive and never seemed to give a second glance to any other woman there, including one of his old girlfriends, who was currently unattached and still extremely attractive.

Cindy had only one really bad moment, and it had nothing to do with any of his past loves but rather with the other woman currently in Nick's life, Madame

Destiny. They were dancing to "You Light Up My Life." The lights had been dimmed, and Cindy's relief at the pleasant way things were turning out had heightened her senses almost to a fever pitch. Nick held her as close as possible, his hands locked together low on her back. Her arms were around his neck, her fingers woven into the thick, blunt line of dark hair at the nape of his neck, her head resting on his shoulder. Their bodies swayed to the melody, but their feet barely moved. Wrapped up in each other the way they obviously were, no one dared intrude, and they were able to dance the whole song together.

"Don't we dance well together?" he murmured against her hair, its reddish highlights brought out by the roving spotlights. "It's odd, but I have the weirdest feeling of déjà vu, dancing with you like this. I know tonight is the first time we've ever danced together, and yet I feel we've done this before. Don't you?"

Cindy couldn't answer without incriminating herself, so she just murmured a noncommittal, "Hmm" against his neck. Mercifully the song ended and the deejay led into "Dancing Queen" by Abba.

"Let's sit this one out. I never did know how to dance to that song. It's not really fast and it's not really slow." Nick kept her hand in his as they left the dance floor and returned to their table where they interrupted a heated discussion about football.

"Hey, here's the old Crimson Mystic himself. I'm sure he remembers what the score was at the Dinwiddie game. Bobby says we beat them twenty-four to fourteen, and I say it was more like thirty-five to fourteen. Tell us, Great Leader, how badly did we stomp Dumb

147

Diddie that year?" one of Nick's fellow alumni asked as soon as Nick and Cindy approached.

"You guys are both wrong," Nick laughed. "The final score was forty-one to fourteen."

"Sure, I remember now. You made one last forty-yard pass after the clock had run out, and Mike caught it in the end zone. Damn, we were good that year."

Cindy remembered that game well. She could have told them the score, the weather on that particular evening at Cameron Field, and the way she had stood in the stands, outwardly cheering for the team but inwardly cheering for the handsome boy who was wearing number twelve on his uniform. It had all been burned into the memory of a young girl who had never dreamed her dearest wish would come true.

The popular songs of the mid-seventies blared in the background, bursts of laughter and boisterous voices occasionally broke through the music, and all the time Cindy kept mentally pinching herself, constantly reassuring herself that she really was here with Nick as her date.

Finally the notes of a slow song faded and was replaced by the strains of "Dear Old PHS," played by the music teacher on the grand piano next to the bar. Many of the attendees in the ballroom joined hands and sang along, amazed that the words could be dredged so easily from the past.

"We're going out for a late-night snack," Mike said, tucking Kay's arm through the circle of his. "Do you guys want to meet us there?"

"No thanks," Nick answered, giving them all a Cheshire-cat grin. "There's something I want to show

Cindy tonight. But I'm sure you two can have a good time without us."

"No doubt about that," Mike said with a chuckle as they all crossed the parking lot to their cars. Kay and Cindy exchanged questioning looks before they split into pairs and drove off into the early-morning darkness.

"What do you want to show me?" Cindy asked.

"You'll see. We're almost there."

"Ah, a surprise. Is it bigger than a bread box?"

"Much. But no more questions because my lips are sealed."

Cindy leaned over the console, kissed the tip of her finger, then outlined his sealed lips, passing the kiss on to him. "Such wonderful lips, it's a shame that they're going to miss out on so much because they can't move."

But his resolve remained firm and he wouldn't speak until they had turned off the main road onto what appeared to be a long private driveway.

"Not another driveway. Really, Nick. I thought you would be more imaginative." Cindy clucked her tongue in pretended dismay.

The car headlights temporarily illuminated the front of a large two-story Colonial house as the car followed the circular drive. But instead of completing the loop and heading back out toward the road, Nick turned beside the house and drove around to the garage in the back. Flipping off the key, the hum of the engine immediately stopped and the silence that followed was complete. It was so quiet, in fact, that when Cindy spoke, she whispered.

"Nick, I don't think anyone's home. Or at least

they're not expecting us. I don't see any lights on in the house."

"I know no one's home because no one lives here. This is a vacant house."

"So what are we doing here?"

"This is my surprise. All week I've been devoting my spare time to finding a suitable house, and this is the one I liked the most. I had planned on showing it to you tomorrow after church, but I can't wait any longer to see your reaction. I really hope you'll be as crazy about it as I am."

"It looks very nice from what I can see in the dark."

"Yes, well, we're going to solve that problem right now," he stated, getting out of the car and moving briskly to open her door. "Come on. Let's go inside and have a look around."

"Do you have the keys?" she asked, hoping it was an unnecessary question.

"No, but that's no problem. When I was here yesterday, I noticed that someone had left the window in the laundry room open just a little. I think that if I can get the screen off, I can climb in, then go around and unlock the back door for you." As he spoke, he took off his sports coat and reached over her to leave it on his seat.

"But Nick, that's breaking and entering," she protested.

"Not really. You see, I've already put earnest money down on this place, so it's almost mine."

"It's that 'almost' that's going to get us into trouble. I don't mind waiting until tomorrow."

Nick's shoulders drooped as his enthusiasm seemed to deflate. "I guess we could wait. But tonight has been so special that I wanted to share my surprise with you now. But if you don't want to—"

Swinging her legs out of the car, she held out her hand and said with a mischievous smile, "You're just determined to get me arrested, aren't you?"

CHAPTER NINE

It took him only a couple of minutes to pry off the screen and slide the window open.

"You did that pretty easily. How many houses have you broken into? Is there something about your past that you should tell me?" Cindy asked dryly, standing back and watching him while keeping an eye on the front of the house in case they were joined by the police. She suspected that if they were caught, the police wouldn't go quite so easily on them this time.

"I'm innocent . . . well, almost. Most of my experience of climbing in windows came from panty raids at college." The last part of his sentence was muffled as he stuck his head in the window, then hoisted his body up and through the opening.

"Thanks for sharing that with me," she muttered, a little disgruntled at the thoughts brought on by his admission.

"The panties were always unoccupied at the time," Nick reassured her laughingly, putting his head back outside long enough to add, "Now go over to the French doors and I'll unlatch them for you."

Cindy obeyed, leaving her lookout post a little reluctantly. It was a cloudy night and the moon offered no assistance as she crossed what she assumed was a patio. The darkness and her unfamiliarity with the surroundings made her very nervous as she cautiously picked her way over the uneven ground, keeping her hand extended in front of her, feeling for unseen obstacles.

A sudden burst of light made her gasp and fall back a few steps until she saw it was coming from the open French door. Clutching her chest, she could feel her heart pounding wildly. If she lived through this courtship, it would be a miracle, she thought.

"Cindy? Where are you?" Nick whispered loudly.

She quickly walked toward him across what she could now see was a beautiful antique brick terrace that led down to a Grecian-style swimming pool. If she had wandered a few dozen feet more to her left, she accidentally would have checked out the launderability of her new silk dress.

"Someone's going to see the lights and turn us in," she said in warning.

"Not as long as we keep the drapes closed. Just look how dark it is out here, and I've already turned on all the lights in this part of the house. Come on. I can't wait for you to see it."

He ushered her into a large den with a vaulted, beamed ceiling that reached to the top of the second story. A balcony from the upstairs hallway stretched the length of the room, and built-in bookcases covered one of the end walls. A beautiful, antique, carved-oak mantel dressed up the brick fireplace that was centered on the back wall between two sets of heavily draped French doors.

"Whoever used to live here must have hated sunshine," she commented, startled at the sound of her voice echoing hollowly in the empty house. Lowering it, she added, "I've never seen drapes that blocked the light as effectively as these."

Their shoes clattered noisily on the polished wood-planked floors as they crossed the den and went into the kitchen. Cindy voiced her approval of the seemingly endless cabinets, the many modern appliances, and the butcher-block island in the middle of the room. They continued their tour through the laundry room, a half bath, and what could have been a sunny breakfast room if drapes hadn't covered every square inch of the arched bay window. Then they went to the formal dining room with an eye-catching crystal chandelier, the formal living room, a small study, and a guest bedroom with its own bathroom.

The upstairs was made up of four of the largest bedrooms Cindy had ever seen, two full bathrooms, and a game room. Except for the draperies and some ugly flocked wallpaper, she absolutely loved the house and told Nick so.

"You really like it?" he persisted.

"Yes, Nick, I do. It's a magnificent house. Maybe it's the style or the woodwork, the six-paneled doors, or those beautiful oak floors downstairs, but it sort of reminds me, on a much smaller scale, of Hickory Hill."

"It did me too. With a little redecorating and a nice mixture of antique and country furniture, I think this could be a very comfortable place to raise a family. Did I tell you that there's seven acres of land that goes with it? And there's also an outdoor hot tub in a gazebo next to the pool and a large workshop."

"I'm sure the workshop will get lots of use since

you're so handy with mechanical things." She couldn't resist joking.

"Well, maybe I'll convert it to a hobby room, or one of my kids might be mechanically inclined enough to fix all those things I can't."

"It's all very nice. How soon do you plan on moving in?"

"The paperwork should be ready as soon as the title search is completed in a couple of weeks. But since I'm paying cash from my trust fund, they've agreed to let me start redecorating right away." They had begun to walk back down the curving staircase into the den. "But there's something very important I need to find out before I give them the final go-ahead to complete the contract."

They had reached the bottom of the stairs, and Nick reached out, his hands lightly gripping her upper arms as he spun her around until she faced him.

"What is it, Nick?" she asked softly.

"I need to know if you like this house well enough to live in it with me." He paused and cleared his throat nervously before continuing. "I guess I'm not doing this very well." Dropping down on one knee in front of her, he lifted her hand to his mouth. Tenderly kissing first the palm of her hand, then the end of her fingers, holding each between his lips for a long, sensuous moment, he stated formally in a voice that cracked with emotion, "Cindy Carroll, I love you very much . . . more than I had ever dreamed I could love anyone. I can't imagine what the rest of my life would be without you, and nothing would make me happier than if you would agree to become my wife."

Cindy had never had a height advantage on Nick,

and looking down at him now was a little disconcerting. She decided to join him at his level. Kneeling down in front of him, she reached out and caressed his cheek, following the square line of his jaw down to his firm chin, then up to his lips. Her fingers lingered there as if by feeling him say the words, they would be more real.

"You're asking me to marry you?" she asked weakly.

"Yes, my love. I know we haven't been dating long, but I feel like we've known each other forever. I don't mean to rush you if you need more time."

More time? She had been waiting more than ten long years for this man even to ask her out for a date. She threw her arms around his neck with such force that he tumbled backward, pulling her with him.

"Oh, yes, Nick. I'll marry you." She laughed, she cried, she covered his face with kisses. Pushing herself up far enough so that she could look into his face, she asked, "Do you think I'm overreacting?"

"Absolutely not," he said, chuckling. "If I had expected a response like this, I would have asked you sooner—and in a more comfortable place." He shifted, stretching his legs out and readjusting her weight on top of him. "Although now that I think about it, we've never been truly alone in a comfortable place."

It suddenly occurred to Cindy that Nick was lying on the floor with almost every inch of his body pressed against hers, and they were, for the first time, absolutely alone in a place that no one would be likely to bother them for quite some time.

Nick realized it, too, and the lighthearted mood instantly changed. The hardwood floor beneath his back might as well have been a featherbed. All he could feel were the soft curves of her breasts pushing against his chest and the sharp bones of her hips rubbing against his, exciting him beyond all reasonable limits of control.

"Cindy?" he began tentatively, wanting and needing to love her completely but waiting for her to give him a sign that she was ready for this next major step in their relationship. This moment in their memories had to be absolutely perfect.

In these days of free-and-easy love it was practically unheard of for a woman to reach the ripe old age of twenty-five without having had several sexual encounters. But Cindy had been raised to value her virtue, waiting for her first experience to be with a man she truly loved . . . and she truly loved Nick.

As she felt her body respond to the suggestiveness of their positions and her desire to stay with Nick, she knew without a doubt that this was it. Beneath her modest, ladylike persona lurked a passionate, sensual woman about to be set free. The intensity of her feelings and physical longings surprised even her, and she could no longer think of any reason to hold back.

Her legs straddled his hips as she sat up, her blazing green eyes still locked to his. Her fingers trailed down the front of his shirt, slowly and sensuously unfastening each button in their path. When she reached the bottom, she pulled the shirt out of his pants, finished unbuttoning it, and let its sides fall back. Spreading her hands over the bare skin of his rib cage, she caressed his heated flesh, delighting in the rough texture of the sprinkling of dark hair that covered his chest and trickled down a narrow path, disappearing beneath his waistband.

The muscles of his stomach tightened beneath her touch until he could bear it no longer. With a sound that was half groan, half sigh, he sat up, scooting her farther down his lap, and wrapped his arms around her. His kisses were gentle yet frenzied, as if he were teetering on the edge. He could no longer hide the powerful effect she had on him, and he knew she could feel it pressing against her. Every time she moved, it brought him closer and closer to the point of no return.

"Love me, Nick," she breathed into his mouth.

His lips sought the pulse point of her neck, and she let her head fall back to give him better access.

"Yes . . . yes," he whispered as his hands found the zipper at the back of her dress. Once unfastened, the bodice fell forward, and his kisses moved down to her bare shoulders and into the tempting shadows beneath. That quickly became too tame as his tongue longed to taste the incredibly soft skin of her breasts and feel the pebbled hardness of her nipples.

She helped him lift her dress and lacy slip over her head, then unclipped her bra and tossed it on top of the pile. She kicked off her shoes, and together they helped her wiggle out of her hose and a tiny pair of bikini panties. As he gazed with smoldering passion at her nude body, Cindy trembled in anticipation. Her breasts felt swollen and heavy, and her desire for him to make love to her was becoming a throbbing ache.

Lifting her off his lap, he shed his own clothes. For several long seconds they allowed their eyes complete freedom.

"You're perfect, just as I had imagined," Nick murmured breathlessly.

"And you're even more magnificent than I had imagined," she answered with a shaky smile.

Again taking her in his arms, they rolled over until he

was lying on top of her. Cupping his hands under her shoulders to cushion them from the hard floor, he pressed a heated kiss on her lips before sliding down far enough so his lips could capture one pink, upturned bud. He drew it deep within his mouth, licking and loving it until he felt her hips begin to squirm beneath his. Turning his attention to her other full, creamy breast, he breathed in the fresh fragrance of her body, magnified now in the heat of her passion.

Her fingers clenched, digging into his back as her hips arched against him. Her breath was coming in ragged gasps and she could feel that her skin was flushed. "Nick . . . oh, Nick . . . please," she cried, unable to take this torment any longer.

His lips returned to hers as his knees parted her legs. He wanted to prolong this moment, to savor it, and bring them both to the highest point of desire possible, but all his good intentions evaporated as he buried himself inside her.

"Cindy!" he cried as he realized how much she was giving him. His momentum slowed, but when her hands stroked his back, moving down to caress his taut buttocks and pull him toward her, encouraging him, he started moving again. Slow at first, the rhythm quickly increased as their passion soared. He heard her startled gasp, and she trembled beneath him as he felt the ripples of satisfaction pull him deeper within her. One final thrust was all it took for him to join her in that wondrous world of ecstasy.

Limply they lay in each other's arms, waiting until the room stopped spinning and they could catch their breath.

"Wow," he said, panting.

"Double wow," she agreed.

"But why didn't you tell me—"

"Shh." She lifted her fingers to his lips. "I love you, Nick, more than anyone or anything. And I'm glad it happened this way."

He sighed and moved off her, stretching out on his back on the cool floor. "But I love you so much. I wasn't prepared. There should have been music and roses and satin sheets. This moment should have been so special."

"It was," she said, reassuring him. Molding her body against his side, she nestled happily in the curve of his arm, resting her head on his shoulder. "This is the most wonderful night of my life. I can't think of a better way to seal our engagement or initiate our new house."

"Are you sure?"

"I'm positive."

"You're not just saying that to make me feel like less of a heel?"

"It was perfect, Nick. Absolutely perfect."

"But I've been so busy looking for this house that I haven't even had time to buy you an engagement ring." He lifted his hand to stroke her hair and noticed the class ring he had dug out of his drawer for the reunion, replacing the one he always wore from the University of Alabama. "Here," he said, tugging it off his finger. Picking up her left hand, he slipped it onto her third finger. "This will have to do until we can go shopping together."

The large ruby-colored stone sparkled in the light as she held her hand up to admire it with as much enthusiasm as if it were the most expensive diamond in the

160

world. But Nick's fingers were much larger than hers, and the heavy gold ring hung loosely around her finger.

"It's a little big." He laughed at the understatement. "At least now I know not to buy you a size-eleven engagement ring. I think two of your fingers would fit in there. But I promise to exchange it for one that will fit you perfectly as soon as possible."

If he only knew how long she had wanted to wear this particular ring, he'd know that the chances of him ever getting it away from her were slim. Cindy remembered envying the other girls in high school who had put tape around their boyfriends' rings to make them fit or had worn them around their neck on a chain. This ring meant more to her than merely a piece of jewelry. It was a sign that her dreams had finally come true. Pulling her own alexandrite ring off her right hand, she slipped it on the same finger to keep Nick's ring from falling off.

"Oh, Nick. I'm so happy," she cried as she gave him a big hug. "I don't want this evening ever to end."

"In that case, will you spend the rest of the night here with me?" he asked, twisting his head to look at her. "I don't want to let you go just yet."

"I'd love to stay," she answered. "But—"

"Wait right here." Nick eased his arm out from under her head and jumped up. Quickly pulling on his slacks, he headed for the door. "I'll be right back. Don't you dare move."

In a few minutes he had returned with a blanket over one arm and a half full bottle of champagne in his hand. Locking the door securely behind him, he dropped the blanket in front of her. "I brought this from the party," he said, holding the champagne aloft, "and I just re-

161

membered that I hadn't taken the blanket out of my trunk since our picnic. Just give me one more minute to turn off the lights down here."

She sat up, watching the lights go out and listening with affectionate amusement to the padding of his bare feet on the wood floors. He was slightly out of breath when he rejoined her in the den, but he surprised her by scooping her up in his arms. Bending down so she could pick up the blanket, he flipped the light switch off with his elbow.

"Where are we going?" she asked, wrapping her arms contentedly around his neck.

"To the master bedroom, of course. It has padded carpeting. My bones are too old for those hard floors." He chuckled, carrying her up the stairs.

"It must be awful to be *that* old. I was hoping that we could—"

"I'm feeling younger already!"

Cindy awoke first the next morning and forced herself to lie perfectly still so she wouldn't wake Nick. It was such an incredible experience to awaken in his arms and be able to stare, unchecked, at his face, so appealingly boyish in sleep. His dark, tousled hair fell across his forehead, much like she remembered it from high school. The blanket had been pushed down to his hips, and her gaze could drink in the sight of the top half of his muscular body.

He yawned, and his eyes fluttered open. Slowly his sleepy blue eyes focused on her, and he gave her a wide, sexy smile.

"Any regrets?" he asked in a voice still husky from sleep.

162

"Only that we can't stay here forever. But it's after ten and I've got to go someplace this afternoon."

"What time this afternoon?" he asked, leaning over and dropping a trail of feathery kisses on the corners of her lips, her eyes, the tip of her nose, and her chin. His hand had been resting on her stomach, but now his fingers began circling her navel, the rings widening and becoming more daring and provocative with each loop.

"Not until two," she murmured breathlessly as she felt a fresh wave of liquid heat rush through her. Though they hadn't gotten much sleep the night before and her body was a little sore from their activities and the hardness of the floor, she wanted all he had to give her. When it came to loving Nick, she was insatiable.

"Do you want to leave now or would you like me to show you how I plan on waking you up every morning after we're married?"

Reaching up to run her hands possessively over the muscles of his bare shoulders, she pulled him closer. *"Every* morning? Won't it look bad when the boss is late to work every day?" she said teasingly.

"I'll send out a memo changing office hours for newlyweds to noon."

And it was close to noon when he finally walked her to the door of her apartment. Cindy turned the knob and was surprised to find that it was locked.

"Kay must still be asleep," she said, but didn't really believe that since she couldn't remember Kay ever sleeping until noon. Taking out her key, she unlocked the door and walked into a dark apartment. Passing Nick a questioning look, she flipped on the light and peeked around the open door into Kay's bedroom. It was empty. "This is Sunday. Maybe she's still at

163

church, or she might have gone out to get something for—" she began, but the sound of someone talking in the hallway made her turn and look expectantly at the front door.

When it swung open and Kay and Mike walked in, still dressed in the same clothes they had been wearing at the reunion, Cindy and Nick exchanged a knowing look.

"So where have you two been all night?" Nick asked in his best fatherly voice.

"We were looking at the moon," Mike retorted good-naturedly.

"I hope you had better luck with it than we did," Nick said with a crooked grin. "And I wouldn't think of mentioning that clouds hid the moon last night."

"Well, it doesn't look like you guys wasted the night, either. I hope you didn't mind having this apartment all to yourselves," Kay said, lifting her eyebrows suggestively.

"Do you mean to tell me that this apartment was *empty* last night?" Cindy squeaked, her hand unconsciously massaging the small of her back. She heard Nick snort, then begin to chuckle. His laughter was infectious, and Cindy joined in, unable to stop as they clung together.

"What on earth is wrong with you guys? Am I missing out on a private joke?" Mike asked with a confused frown.

"You had to have been there." Nick gasped, and when his twinkling eyes met Cindy's, they both broke down in a renewed fit of laughter. "But I'm glad you weren't."

The two men finally left after deciding to change

164

clothes, get some lunch, and spend the afternoon on the tennis court. And because they were both running so late, Cindy and Kay had to work very quickly to turn Cindy into Madame Destiny in time for her visit to the children's hospital that afternoon.

Kay was enthusiastic about Cindy's engagement and found a gold chain long enough so Cindy could wear Nick's ring around her neck and keep it tucked inside her dress where no one would be able to see it.

"How did he take it when you told him you were Madame Destiny?" Kay asked as she finished brushing the straight black wig and pinned it in place on top of Cindy's head.

"I haven't yet. The subject just hasn't come up."

"And it won't unless you bring it up," Kay warned. "Anyway, I won't be here when you get home this afternoon." Kay glanced at her watch and groaned. "I'm supposed to be at the theater in fifteen minutes to help with the matinee performance. Then Mike is going to pick me up there, and we're going to go out to eat or something, so I'll be home late."

"So things went well last night?" Cindy asked with a friendly wink.

"Things went great! Maybe we can make it a double wedding." Kay returned her wink, then continued, "But I've got to leave now. Can you finish by yourself?"

"Sure. Have fun."

The kids were adorable and made a wonderful audience while Madame Destiny told them fairy tales about unicorns and beautiful princesses falling in love with handsome princes. Though Cindy had told the same stories many times before, never had she been able to tell them with such enthusiasm and conviction. Her life was living proof that fairy tales *could* come true. She wasn't exactly a beautiful princess, but she had found her handsome prince, and they would marry and live happily ever after.

It was almost five o'clock when she parked her car back at her apartment building. She yawned and rolled her head around in circles to relax her tight neck muscles. She was exhausted but wondrously happy. Maybe a nice long soak in a tub of hot water would revive her, or even a short nap. Nick wasn't supposed to pick her up until seven, so she had a couple of hours to rest up.

No one was in the hallway, so she darted from the stairs to her door, quickly fitting the key into the lock. But as soon as she turned it, she realized that the door hadn't been locked. Love must be making her forgetful, she thought to herself, because she was almost certain she had checked that the door was locked when she left.

Anxious to get out of the dress and into the tub, she practically stumbled into the living room but stopped short when she saw who was sitting on her couch. The time was obviously right to tell Nick the truth, because there he was, staring incredulously at her, as if he were seeing a ghost.

CHAPTER TEN

"Madame Destiny?"

"Nick?"

"Cindy!"

Nick jumped to his feet and was standing just inches in front of her. The confusion was clear in his eyes as his gaze slowly swept her figure from the top of her head to the tips of her toes, then back up again until it settled on her face.

She had pushed back the veil for the drive home and had an unobstructed view of his expression. She watched helplessly as his bewilderment was replaced by fury until his eyes turned a cold, icy blue, so unlike the warm, friendly color they usually were.

"How did you get in? Did I forget to lock the door?" She forced her voice to sound natural, but the upward thrust of her chin showed that she was trying not to be put on the defensive.

"Your landlady recognized me and let me in with her passkey when I asked if it would be all right to wait in here for you."

"But what are you doing here? I wasn't expecting you for a couple of hours."

"That's obvious." His hands clenched as he felt an

almost uncontrollable urge to yank the black wig off her head. Instead he thrust his fists deep into his pockets and began to pace restlessly. "Don't you think you owe me an explanation?" he demanded.

"Yes, of course I do. You see, I sometimes dress up like this, as Madame Destiny, to go to charity functions and—"

"Butt into people's lives," he said, interrupting her and finishing her sentence for her.

"No, I just read their palms and tell them—"

"Whatever strikes your fancy, regardless of the consequences."

"No, please let me explain," she pleaded.

"Here," he growled, his nostrils flaring as he pulled his left hand out of his pocket and thrust it in front of her face. "Show me exactly where it says how gullible I am. Show me my stupidity line."

"Nick, I—"

"Lord, how pleased you must have felt with yourself. You planned this whole thing so well. And I played along with you like a real chump, didn't I? You had me right where you wanted. Although God only knows why you wanted me so much."

"Because I love you, Nick." She sobbed, reaching out to grasp the front of his shirt. "I wanted to be your wife."

Angrily he knocked her hands away and moved back until the couch was between them. "Are all the women in the world the same? Is money and status all they think about? I wish my father hadn't died and I had never inherited this company. From now on I'll never be able to know if a woman loves me for myself or because she knows I have a lot of damn money."

"Nick, I didn't plan to deceive you. It just sort of happened. I meant to tell you the truth."

"Sure you did," he replied with a dry, humorless laugh. "That's why you danced with me at the charity ball as Madame Destiny and let me tell you how crazy I was about you—or rather about Cindy. I seem to be having a little trouble keeping the two of you separate."

"I couldn't tell you then. I was afraid you'd leave me."

"So you just fed me lines about how *perfect* 'Cindy' was for me." He shook his head. "Those brown contact lenses and high heels threw me way off track. When I think of how you tricked me, telling me all those things about my accident and my business, my girlfriends and my children. Do you realize that I've rearranged my whole life because of what you told me? I broke up with Felicia. I put money down on a house large enough for my *five* kids. Lord, what a fool I've been."

"No, you haven't. I didn't mean it that way at all. I just wanted you to notice me."

"Well, I've noticed you, *madame,* and now, if you'll give me back my ring, I'll tell you good-bye." His eyes narrowed, and he leaned toward her, resting his hands on the back of the couch. "I came here early today because Don called and has given his notice. I couldn't wait to give you the good news that you were about to be promoted to personnel director, but now, considering the circumstances, I feel it would be best if you looked for another job with a different company. I'll give you a good reference, because no one knows better than me how *good* you really are."

Without even thinking about it she reached out and slapped him solidly across his cheek. She watched with mixed horror and a certain amount of satisfaction as a perfect outline of her hand reddened the tanned perfection of his face.

"I didn't deserve that remark," she stated calmly. "I only did what I did because I love you. You're going to think this is really corny, but I've loved you ever since I was fourteen years old. I thought you were the most wonderful boy in the world." She fumbled with the chain, pulling it up until the ring popped out from under her high, lacy collar. Her fingers shook as she released the clasp and slid the ring off the chain. "Here's your precious ring. I must have been mistaken about you. I thought you had grown up. I thought there was more to you than the playboy jock, the poor little rich boy that all my friends told me you were. I thought there were real human feelings beneath that handsome shell."

"You're the one who's a phony," he retorted hotly. "How many faces do you have? You must spend your spare time working at the theater with Kay because you're one hell of an actress."

"I never pretended my love for you," she said in a voice so low, he had to strain to hear it. "That was very real. I thought we had something really special. We could have been so happy together, but you don't care enough about me even to try to understand my side of the story."

"How do I know what I feel for you?" he bellowed. "I don't even know who you are! You're the one with all the answers. You're the magnificent—or is that the manipulative?—Madame Destiny. So show me how great you are. Why don't *you* tell me what I feel. That's what you've been doing since the very beginning of our relationship." He snatched the ring from her outstretched hand, glared at her, and strode across the room to the door. "Well, read your own palm and see if it says that I'm fixing to walk out of your life forever. For once you'll be right."

Cindy flinched as the door slammed behind him. All the spirit left her body, and she fell limply onto the couch. What had gone wrong? It had all happened so fast. They had both said such ugly, unkind things to each other. How had it ended so quickly?

The last few weeks, and especially the previous night, had been so beautiful that she never would have imagined things could change so abruptly. What had happened to the easygoing man with twinkling blue eyes and laughing, delightful lips? He was supposed to have understood her dilemma and reassured her that it didn't matter how it had happened as long as they had gotten together. This should have been one of those hilarious memories that they shared with their children and grandchildren.

Of course, there was no chance of that now. Only an hour ago she had been hearing wedding bells. Now she had lost not only her lover and her fiancé, but also her job.

Kay's chain was still clenched in her hand, and as Cindy stretched open her fingers she stared down at the strange design of curves and crisscrossing lines that had been added to her own natural pattern. Nick was wrong about her not being able to read palms. It was clear even to an inexperienced eye that her life was in an awful mess.

She sat for several more minutes, trying to sort out her thoughts, but the apartment seemed to be closing in

171

on her. She had to get away for a few days, breathe some fresh air, see some new sights, and maybe apply for a few jobs. While her bathwater was running, Cindy called her secretary and, without going into any details, told her that Don would not be back, that Cindy would be taking a week of vacation, and to handle things as best she could at the office.

Cindy undressed, carefully hanging up the gown and pinning the wig on a faceless Styrofoam head. After her bath she packed a suitcase with some casual clothes and hung a couple of businesslike outfits for interviews in a garment bag. She then made one more call to get reservations, typed out a letter of resignation, which she sealed in an envelope to mail at the nearest box, and scribbled a note of explanation to Kay before leaving the apartment and Petersburg behind.

She drove her little yellow car through Hopewell and across the James River on the Benjamin Harrison Bridge, then turned north toward Richmond. It didn't take her long to find the cutoff that led to Hickory Hill, and she followed the curving road through the trees until the plantation house came into view. She had been lucky they had an opening, the young girl who was dressed in a pre-Civil War outfit remarked as she led Cindy up to a single room on the third floor.

But as soon as Cindy had unpacked her clothes, placing them neatly in the drawers of an antique chest or hanging them inside a tall mirrored wardrobe, reality began to set in. She didn't feel very lucky. She had gone for the big one, the perfect dream, and when she lost, she had lost it all.

Alone with her sorrow, she no longer had to be brave or strong. Unconsciously she had been holding the tears back, but now, with all her defenses dropped, the tears came. Her eyes filled as deep, racking sobs shook her body and she fell down across the feather mattress of the bed. She cried for the love they had shared and the love they would never know. She cried for her frustrated past and her bleak future.

It hurt like heck to lose a dream.

Feeling thoroughly sorry for herself, she finally drifted off to sleep. Her emotions had been through such turmoil over the past twenty-four hours, followed by the cleansing flood of tears, that she slept with the soundness of a child. Her busy schedule and all her late nights had caught up with her, and she barely moved for the next twelve hours.

She was totally disoriented when she finally did awaken. For several confusing minutes her gaze floated around the room, seeing but not recognizing the eyelet lace curtains that held back none of the early-morning sun's rays, the graceful oak furniture, the rosebud wallpaper that stretched up to the unusually tall ceiling, and the oval, framed pictures of horses and people she didn't know. Looking down at herself, she saw that she was still dressed in the slacks and pullover sweater she had been wearing the day before.

Her stomach growled, reminding her that she hadn't eaten since the buffet at the reunion, and that seemed like ages ago. All of which served to remind her why she was there and why her eyes were so swollen and scratchy. She felt completely empty, as if her entire past life had been wiped out.

Physically she should have been rested and energetic after all that sleep. Instead her total lack of motivation was more debilitating than exhaustion. She simply did not know where to go or what to do next, not just for the rest of her life but even for the rest of the day. There was no one waiting for her, no job she must do. She had no plans or goals. She didn't even have to leave the room if she didn't want to. It was a very strange realization.

Lethargically she remained on the bed, lying on her back and watching the patterns on the ceiling made by sunbeams peeking through the eyelet holes in the curtains. She had no more tears left to cry. Her emotions felt completely drained, leaving her open and vulnerable. For quite some time she didn't move.

Cindy tried not to think about Nick because she certainly didn't need to be any more depressed, but that's exactly where her thoughts wandered. She wished she hadn't called him a playboy jock or a poor little rich boy, because she knew he wasn't any of those things. He was a sweet, sensitive man who was still going through a major adjustment in his life. He hadn't yet learned how to handle the pressures and demands of the family business, much less the added responsibilities of a personal relationship. She had just shoved her way into his life at a time when he wasn't ready for any more surprises.

Her stomach growled again, and she needed to find the bathroom. Her guide last night had explained that all four bedrooms in this wing had to share one bathroom as she had pointed vaguely down the hall. Cindy wished she had been paying a little more attention. It was only these unignorable needs that finally got her off the bed.

Force of habit made her take her toothbrush and her cosmetic bag with her. Running her fingers through her hair in a halfhearted attempt to tidy it, she stepped out into the hallway. Luckily there was only one door slightly ajar, and she went inside, locking it behind her.

It was a large bathroom, complete with a deep claw-foot tub and an old-fashioned pull-chain toilet. A beveled mirror hung over the lavatory, and when she looked in it, Cindy was horrified by her own reflection. Her face was pale, her eyes were red and puffy, and her hair looked like it hadn't been brushed in a month. A sense of pride overcame her apathy, and she went to work to make herself look presentable.

Returning to her room, she changed into a pair of shorts and a cotton shirt. Slipping on a pair of sandals, she decided it was silly to stay in her room now that she was completely dressed, so she went downstairs to the restaurant. It was Monday, but there were still a good number of tourists there, either spending the night or going on the tour. And since it was close to lunchtime, there weren't many empty tables.

Instead of one large room the restaurant was comprised of what used to be the mansion's dining room, ballroom, and drawing room. Each area was elegantly furnished and had dozens of potted plants placed in the corners and in front of the fireplace. A hostess dressed in a long, full-skirted period costume, seated Cindy at a small table for two near a window and gave her a menu.

Cindy didn't want to be hungry. She thought it would be much more dramatically appropriate to grieve and waste away over her lost love. When her plate arrived, filled with thick slices of Virginia ham, candied yams, and black-eyed peas, she decided she would just pick at her food and eat enough tiny, ladylike bites to keep her alive. To her surprise, by the time she stopped chewing, the plate was clean and she had even devoured a piece of homemade pecan pie.

This was not the proper way to grieve, she thought with disgust. It was even more upsetting when she realized that by getting dressed and eating a good meal, things no longer looked so hopeless. Apparently she just was not cut out to be a simpering Southern belle. She was more of the Scarlett O'Hara type, always able to get back on her feet and try to make it to the ever-elusive "tomorrow."

Feeling much better about herself, she set out for a tour of the stables. One of her guides had mentioned there was horseback riding, and she thought she might check into that.

The next few days were lazy but full as she joined in with the activities at the plantation. There were several horses available to the tourists for hourly rentals, but the overnight guests could take them out for as long as they wanted. Cindy spent many hours in the saddle of a small, snowy white Arabian mare named Shiloh. Together they explored every square inch of the grounds, basking under the warm summer sun.

She went fishing in the river, played croquet on the back lawn with some of the other overnighters, and took long walks through the fields that had once grown cotton and tobacco but now were covered with wildflowers. It was a return to the simple life, a slower pace. It was very peaceful and quiet and rejuvenating. Slowly her spirits and self-esteem began to rebuild.

By Friday she had decided that she had nothing to lose by calling Nick. He had had as much time to think things over as she had. Maybe he had changed his mind about her. After all, her biggest crime had been an error in judgment and timing. Surely those weren't unforgivable offenses. Possibly he had missed her as much as she was missing him and was waiting anxiously for her call. She had talked to Kay a couple of times during the week, but her friend hadn't been able to give her a clue as to what to expect. Neither she nor Mike had seen or heard from Nick.

It was two in the afternoon, so she knew he should be at the office. Dialing the familiar number, she greeted the switchboard operator and asked to speak to Nick. Eagerly, and even a little impatiently, she waited while the connection was made to his office. But instead of Nick his secretary answered.

"Hi, Marianne. May I speak to Nick, please?"

"Oh, hi, Cindy. How are you enjoying your vacation?"

"It's nice. I'm getting caught up on my sleep. Is Nick in his office?" she persisted, anxious to hear his deep, sexy voice.

"Uh . . . yes, he is. But he asked me to hold all his calls. He's interviewing for a new personnel director."

"Oh." Her hand tightened on the telephone receiver until her knuckles turned white. He was already replacing her in his company. He had probably already replaced her in his love life too.

"Cindy, are you still there? Mr. Wainwright told me you had turned in your notice. Have you found another job yet?"

She had to swallow several times to push the lump in her throat far enough down so she could speak. Fighting hard to keep from losing her newly bolstered self-confidence, she responded with a casual, "Oh, sure. That's what I was calling to tell Nick . . . er, Mr.

Wainwright, about. Would you pass the message on to him for me?"

"Certainly. And I'm glad to hear about your new job. We really miss you around here, but we were sure that with your experience and personality it wouldn't take you long to find something."

"Yes, well, I'll be by one day next week to clean out my desk. Bye." Cindy had to say the last few words rapidly so she could get off the phone before Marianne could hear the tears in her voice. It really was all over. There was no going back now. Her bridges had all been burned behind her. Her eyes remained strangely dry, but that annoying lump in her throat seemed to be growing, choking her.

Without conscious thought her feet led her across the backyard to the stables. One of the stable boys saddled Shiloh for her, and soon she was cantering away from the mansion. Thunderclouds were building on the horizon, and the approaching storm cooled the air. She could smell the rain in the wind that whipped against her face. She rode on until she was on the far boundaries of the plantation when the first wet drops began to fall. There was no place to take shelter except under one of the huge trees, but the distant rumble of thunder told her that wouldn't be a very good idea. She decided she would have to return to the stable as quickly as possible and hope she could beat out the brunt of the storm.

The mare gave her wholehearted approval to the plan and stretched out in a ground-consuming gallop back across the pastures. They beat the lightning, but the downpour of rain caught them just before they reached the stables. Cindy and the horse were dripping wet when she finally dismounted and led the animal into the welcomed warmth.

"I'm sorry," she apologized to the stable boy as she helped him unsaddle and wipe down the mare. "I saw the clouds, but I didn't think the storm would hit us so quickly."

"Neither did I, or I wouldn't have let you go." He gave her a shy but reassuring smile. "It wasn't your fault. These afternoon showers are unpredictable. I can finish with Shiloh. You'd better go inside and dry yourself off. There's nothing worse than a summer cold."

She didn't try to explain that she was a native to the area and should have known better than to get caught in a thunderstorm. It would have been Nick's fault if she had been struck by lightning. If she hadn't been so preoccupied by the disturbing news she had received on the phone, she would have realized it wasn't an ideal time for riding across an open field.

Dripping wet, she quickly gathered dry clothes and went to the bathroom. In the short time that she had been here she had fallen in love with the bathtub. It was perfect for long, lazy soaks in neck-deep water, which proved to be very conducive for reflective meditation. Unfortunately the tub was not there for her sole use and she had to be considerate of the other guests.

But her mind was full, and she needed some extra time to sort things out. The gallop through the rain had given her emotions time to cool. Now her logic began to return by reminding her of all the good times she and Nick had had together. Regardless of what he thought right now, they had been perfectly suited for each other. Sure, she had stepped out of line a little by setting the two of them up, but she had let him take over from there . . . except for the ball. But maybe someday he would be able to understand that she had still been unsure of their relationship then, especially when he had showed up with Felicia.

She squeezed some shampoo out of the bottle and worked it into a lather on her head as she continued her little pep talk. So what if she had lost a job? That was unfortunate but not fatal. She could find another one. But losing Nick was something else entirely. He might be able to replace her in the office, but she was convinced that he would never find another woman who suited him so well and loved him so much.

Since when was she the type of woman to roll over and play dead just because a little obstacle had popped up? If she had let herself be intimidated by a little adversity, she never would have gotten as far as she had. She never would have been adventurous enough to let herself be talked into becoming Madame Destiny or the nerve to make up such a crazy idea as the woman-in-the-blue-dress-making-coffee story. She had waited ten years for him; she could surely be patient enough to wait a few more months. She might have blown her chances with him forever, but she would never know unless she tried.

PHS never knew what they had missed, she thought with a merry chuckle. She would have made a darn good cheerleader. Look what a terrific job she had done on herself. Thoroughly depressed when she had left the stables, tired and confused when she had gotten into the tub but full of hopes and plans when she got out. Humming to herself, she towel-dried her hair, then combed the tangles out of it.

It was only a few minutes after seven o'clock, but it

180

was still raining outside, which made it seem later. Cindy decided it was too much trouble to get redressed, so she called down to the restaurant and asked them to send up some dinner. Slipping out of her robe, she put on an apricot-colored shorty gown and had just finished polishing her toenails a gaudy scarlet that would have made Madame Destiny envious when there was a knock at her door.

"Room service," a voice called from the hallway.

Cindy opened the door, carefully keeping most of her scantily clad body behind it. She smiled at the college girl who had brought her dinner to her.

"Thanks, Jody. It looks delicious," Cindy said as she took the tray. "Would you put it on my bill?"

"Sure thing. But there's one more thing." Jody reached into one of the huge pockets on the front of her apron and pulled out a football. "There's a man downstairs that said to give you this."

"A football? A man downstairs?" Cindy repeated.

"He wants to know if he can come up here and see you. I told him he'd have to wait until I talked to you. He looks pretty weird."

Cindy was getting more confused by the second. For just an instant she had thought the man might be Nick. But why would he send her a football? And as far as she was concerned, he was the most attractive man in the world, certainly not weird-looking. It just didn't make sense.

"I'm not expecting any visitors, Jody. The man probably has me confused with someone else."

"That's what I thought. I'll tell him that you can't see him."

"Of course she will see me," a masculine voice

boomed from the hallway, causing both Jody and Cindy to jump. "I'm the Crimson Mystic and I've come to tell her fortune." A tall, dark figure leapt into the doorway, an ankle-length crimson cape swirling theatrically around him. Both women stared wide-eyed at the imposing yet bizarre sight of the man dressed in a football uniform beneath the rustling cape, standing statue-still in a perfect superhero pose.

"I'm sorry. I told you he was weird," Jody apologized to Cindy. "I didn't realize he had followed me up here. I'll call the sheriff and get him to send a patrol car out here."

"No!" Both Cindy and the Crimson Mystic shouted in unison.

"I mean, uh, that won't be necessary," Cindy added in a calmer voice. "I know this man, or I think I know him. It's okay if he stays."

"Are you sure?" Jody asked, eyeing the man doubtfully.

"Yes, it will be all right."

"Okay." Jody shrugged. "Here's your football," she said, handing it to the man and backing out of the room.

"Nick, what are you doing here?" Cindy's heart fluttered in her chest, and she quickly set the dinner tray down on the dresser.

"Nick? Who is this Nick?" the man drawled in an exaggerated Southern accent. "I am the Crimson Mystic and I have brought along my crystal football to tell your future."

He was leaving her no option but to play along, which she was more than willing to do. Obviously he had gone to a lot of trouble to create this scene, and she wanted to see him play it out. Besides, it was so wonderful having him here, for whatever reason, that she would have agreed to almost anything. She only wished she had had some warning so she could have fixed her hair and dressed in something a little fancier than a nightie. But Nick never seemed to catch her at her best.

"Okay, Mystic. I've been having a little trouble with my life lately," she said solemnly. She glanced around the room. There was no place to sit except on the bed. "I guess we'll have to sit here while you tell me what I should expect in my future." She plopped down on the foot of her bed and patted the quilted space in front of her.

For the first time since he had appeared, the Crimson Mystic looked a little disconcerted. His grip on the football tightened, but he moved across the room and joined her, somewhat gingerly, on the bed. With a great flourish he placed the football between them and circled his hands over it.

"I see that you are an efficient, diligent worker who has just quit her job—"

"Was fired from her job," Cindy said, correcting him.

"Whatever." He dismissed her words with a wave. "I see that if you still want your job back, the boss has had second thoughts and would welcome you with open arms."

"But I thought the boss was interviewing for my replacement today."

"Absolutely not. I see that he was interviewing to find someone to fill your old job as assistant, but he just couldn't bring himself to accept your resignation until he has had one more chance to talk to you."

"Now that's odd," Cindy said thoughtfully. "I was

under the impression that my boss never wanted to see me again. And the reason I believe this is because he told me so in those exact words."

"Well, your boss has had time to reconsider the situation and realizes he acted a little hastily."

"Hastily?" she echoed. She refused to make this easy for him. "Does this mean that I've been unfired?"

"Shh. You're breaking the Crimson Mystic's concentration. As if he weren't having enough trouble as it is," he said, glancing toward her bare, shapely legs, which were tucked Indian-style in front of her.

"Sorry, but as you know, I wasn't expecting to entertain a guest tonight."

"The Crimson Mystic is glad to hear that." The first hint of a smile tugged at the corners of his mouth. Turning his attention back to his football, he stared down intensely at the scuffed brown pigskin and continued, "I also see that there is a man in your life who loves you very much. I see him down on his knees first to propose and then to apologize."

Cindy leaned forward and squinted down at the ball. "This I've got to see. Show me where you're seeing this. I've had some experience with these things, and I know how exciting it is to get these visions."

"It's right there, as plain as the freckle on your . . . uh . . ." He paused, dragging his gaze away from the tantalizing view of well-rounded breasts that fell forward against her gown when she leaned toward him like that. "Uh," he repeated, swallowing hard. "Right there," he insisted. "Perhaps you haven't worked with as many footballs as I have and can't see it as clearly, but I assure you it's there."

"I guess I'll just have to take your word for it. Anyway, tell me more about this man who loves me. Does he have a name?"

"Right now his name is Mud, but he is hoping that you will forgive him and take him back. His life has been very boring and empty since you left."

"But can he forgive and forget that I didn't tell him the whole truth? Does he understand that I did what I did because I'm wild about him? Does he realize that I meant well and am not the least bit interested in his business or his money?"

"Yes, he does. As soon as he cooled down enough to think sensibly, he realized he had overreacted. It was just that he was so disappointed to think that the woman he loved had tricked him. His masculine pride was hurt because he felt like she had taken unfair advantage of the situation to make him do what she wanted. But he doesn't care what happened before. He just knows that he misses her and wants her and loves her with all his heart."

"Show me," she whispered.

With a flip of his hand he tossed the football across the room and closed the space between them. Cupping her face, he leaned over and let his lips slowly and sensuously explore hers. The tip of his tongue followed the sensitive inner curve of her mouth before slipping between her teeth to meet and mate with her tongue.

A sigh of complete satisfaction escaped from her mouth into his. Her arms wrapped around his neck and her fingers buried themselves in the thick silkiness of his dark hair. It seemed like ages since he had kissed her, and she felt an immediate and powerful surge of desire heat her blood. By mutual, unspoken consent, they moved closer until her breasts were pressed against the solid, plastic curves of his shoulder pads.

After several more minutes of getting reacquainted, they separated, temporarily satisfying themselves with staring deeply into each other's eyes.

"Tell me. Do you still love this man?" he asked, his voice husky.

"Forget that man. After kisses like those I've fallen in love with you," she teased with a gentle smile. "I always have been a sucker for a guy in a football uniform."

"I hate to disappoint you, but the Crimson Mystic is already in love with someone else, a gorgeous brunette named Madame Destiny."

"That's nice. She's a good friend of mine and she needs a man like you to spice up her life."

"Have you noticed that this room has suddenly started to get real crowded?" he asked with a warm chuckle. "Do you think we could tell the Mystic and the Madame to get lost long enough for Nick and Cindy to get engaged again? I just happen to have brought along a couple of rings with me, in case you didn't slam the door in my face before we could talk."

"I love you, Nick. I've always loved you and I always will."

"And I love you, my cute, adorable woman." He dropped another kiss on her uplifted lips. "Do you think the people who run this place would care if I checked in for the weekend?"

"But you'll miss the Fourth of July picnic."

"They don't need me there. As long as the food and beer arrives on time, they'll probably have more fun without me. Of course, they won't have as good a softball team without you."

"I've learned how to play a mean game of croquet since I've been here. Next year we'll have to play that at the picnic."

"Oh, sure, I can just see the guys in the factory playing croquet." He laughed. "Actually I have a different sort of team sport in mind for us this weekend. If you'll help me take off this darn football uniform, we can start practicing for those five kids you promised me. And if you don't mind, I'd like them all to be boys so I can train them for the PHS football team. It's about time they had another Wainwright on the field."

"Five kids." Cindy groaned. "Let me look at your palm again and see if maybe I didn't read that wrong."

"Later, my love. Later."

Now you can reserve April's

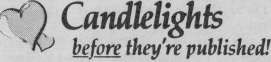

Candlelights

before they're published!

♥ You'll have copies set aside for *you*
  the instant they come off press.
♥ You'll save yourself precious shopping
  time by arranging for *home delivery*.
♥ You'll feel proud and efficient about
  organizing a system that *guarantees* delivery.
♥ You'll avoid the disappointment of not
  finding *every* title you want and need.

ECSTASY SUPREMES $2.75 each

☐ 165 ADVENTURE WITH A STRANGER,
   Donna Kimel Vitek 10046-1
☐ 166 LOVERS AND LIARS, Deborah Sherwood 14994-0
☐ 167 THE PERFECT EXCHANGE, Andrea St. John . . .16855-4
☐ 168 THE GENTLEMAN FARMER, Lynn Patrick 12836-6

ECSTASY ROMANCES $2.25 each

☐ 498 KNIGHT OF ILLUSIONS, Jane Atkin 14596-1
☐ 499 DARE THE DEVIL, Elaine Raco Chase 11759-3
☐ 500 TICKET TO A FANTASY, Terri Herrington 18679-X
☐ 501 INTIMATE PERSUASION, Alice Bowen 14120-6
☐ 502 CASANOVA'S DOWNFALL, Betty Henrichs 10982-5
☐ 503 MYSTERY AT MIDNIGHT, Eve O'Brian 15989-X
☐ *12 THE TEMPESTUOUS LOVERS,*
   Suzanne Simmons 18551-3
☐ *18 SWEET EMBER, Bonnie Drake* 18459-2

At your local bookstore or use this handy coupon for ordering:

**DELL READERS SERVICE—DEPT. B1440A
6 REGENT ST., LIVINGSTON, N.J. 07039**

Please send me the above title(s) I am enclosing $ _____ (please add 75¢ per copy to cover
postage and handling) Send check or money order—no cash or CODs Please allow 3-4 weeks for shipment

Ms /Mrs /Mr _____

Address _____

City/State _____ Zip _____